He eyed the bright, festive, oversized flowers. "This place never changes." Jake took his menu but laid it aside, already knowing what he planned to order. Tori did the same.

"So, it's Monday, and you're here, not at school." His eyes roamed over the bright potted plants, Mexican tile, and bright Mexico décor.

"Luckily I'm on spring break—otherwise this wedding week would prove difficult. Roni planned a full schedule."

The waitress breezed by, stopping to take their order. She grabbed the menus and disappeared.

"I like the way they are doing this prewedding week. Lots of activities and time to spend together."

"Roni hates that so often your closest friends fly in, hit the rehearsal dinner, attend the wedding, and fly out. She didn't want it to feel rushed. Of course, not everyone can come for the whole week."

"I'm glad I could. And you, too, for that matter." He winked at the cute blond seated across from him and found himself looking forward to spending time getting to know Tori better. Who knew, but maybe by the end of the week he'd convince her to come to Idaho and work for him this summer. He needed an accounts payable clerk for Allison's two-month maternity leave, and since Tori taught basic accounting, she just might fit the resort's needs. And his. . .

JERI ODELL is a native of Tucson, Arizona. She has been married almost thirty-seven years and has three wonderful adult children and five precious grandchildren. Jeri holds family dear to her heart, second only to God. This is Jeri's ninth novel for Heartsong Presents. She has also written several novellas, a nonfiction book, and articles on family issues for several Christian publications. She thanks God for the privilege of writing for Him. When not writing or reading, she is busy working in the finance office of her church. If you'd like, you can e-mail her at Jeri.Odell@gmail.com.

Books by Jeri Odell

HEARTSONG PRESENTS
HP413—Remnant of Victory
HP467—Hidden Treasures
HP525—Game of Pretend
HP595—Surrendered Heart
HP781—Always Yesterday
HP805—Only Today
HP825—Until Tomorrow
HP906—Perfect Ways

Perfect Peace

Jeri Odell

Heartsong Presents

I dedicated my first book to you and now, twenty books later, you are still my high school sweetheart and the man I want to grow old with. I love you—forever and a day. Your Sweetie.

A note from the Author:
I love to hear from my readers! You may correspond with me by writing:

Jeri Odell
Author Relations
PO Box 721
Uhrichsville, OH 44683

ISBN 978-1-61626-079-8

PERFECT PEACE

Our mission is to publish and distribute inspirational products offering exceptional value and biblical encouragement to the masses.

PRINTED IN THE U.S.A.

prologue

January 1

Tori Wade laid her well-worn copy of *Pride and Prejudice* in her lap, stretched her arms toward heaven, and yawned. It was the first book she read each new year. She uncurled her slender, pajama-clad legs and stood, glancing at her watch. "Only five past nine." She sighed. Some evenings dragged on forever and tonight definitely did.

Her blue cell phone, lying on the coffee table, vibrated to life. Tori grabbed it, hoping to see Spense's picture smiling up at her from the screen. No such luck. It was Roni's name that popped up. It drove her sister crazy that Tori sat home alone nearly every weekend since her best friend Jen had left for Italy. She settled back on the mocha-colored couch, propping her feet on the dark wood coffee table, and opened her phone. "Hey."

"Tors—whatcha doing? Reading or grading papers?"

"At the moment, I'm missing Spense and contemplating a hot bath, followed by a movie in bed."

"Ah, the good life," her twin mocked. "It's Friday night and New Year's Day! You live like an old spinster."

"Being home alone on most weekends is certainly the downside of an engagement to a man living a few thousand miles away. And a BFF in Italy. Ah, but Spense is worth it."

"He is gorgeous—that Mr. T. D. and H. of yours."

"No argument here. He is tall, dark, and handsome." How

5

he'd fallen for her—the lesser twin, not as good at anything as Roni—she'd never know. "He's eye candy for sure, but it's his voice that makes my heart thump." Just thinking about it caused a shiver to race down her back.

"That rich baritone, huh? He does have the perfect voice for a newscaster, but enough about your prince charming. I think I just met one of my own!" Roni's excitement danced through the airwaves and touched Tori.

She smiled, shaking her head at Roni's glee. Her sister had not had much luck with men—though there had been plenty interested. "Spill." Strangely, Tori had been the successful one in the man department. Sure, she got off to a slow start, but in college God sent Spense in her direction, and it had been bliss ever since.

"He's not as gorgeous as Spense, but he is a viable hunk of man. I want you to come to the fellowship hall tonight so you can meet him."

"Tonight?" Tori glanced down at her pink and green plaid pajamas. "Are you nuts?"

The doorbell rang. Tori glanced across her living room at her front door, then back at her phone. "Are you at my door? Did you drag him over here?"

"No. I told you I'm at church."

"It would not be unlike you to show up at my door, new viable man in tow," Tori reminded her as she peeked through the peephole on her apartment door.

"Spense!" she squealed. "Gotta go." She shut her phone and shoved it in the front pocket of her flannel pajama top while simultaneously throwing the door wide open.

Her heart pounded and excitement shot through her veins. She leapt into his arms, wrapping hers tightly around his waist. "You came to celebrate the New Year with me. I can't believe how thoughtful you are! Thank you, thank you, thank you. You are the best surprise ever."

Loosening her hold, she stood on tiptoes and planted a kiss on his tanned cheek. Leaning back, she gazed upon his perfect face—the face she loved dearly.

"Tori. . ."

She pulled his head toward her until their lips met. His kiss never failed to send her heart soaring somewhere into the clouds. But tonight it felt distant. His lips were cool and unresponsive against hers.

Reluctantly she ended the kiss, grabbed his hand, and pulled him into her apartment, shutting the door behind them. "Did you get a hotel, or do you want to stay in my parents' guest room?"

He shoved his hands into his jacket pockets, not answering her question. Something was amiss. His charcoal eyes roamed around the apartment but never rested on her.

A blanket of fear settled over her. "Spense?" Her mouth suddenly felt dry, and her heart sank. The distance that had grown between them in the past few months suddenly filled her with insecurity. She'd convinced herself he was busy in his new position as news anchor at KTMN in Minneapolis, but now she wondered if he'd used the job as an excuse not to call.

She needed to sit, but could her legs carry her to the chair? They felt weak, like they were filled with Jell-O instead of bone and muscle. She leaned back against the front door, gripping the handle for some semblance of support.

"Are you sick? Did something happen to your parents? What's wrong?" *Please let it be anything but us*. He hadn't said "I love you" in months unless she said it first. That fact bothered her before, but now it suddenly terrified her.

He turned slightly, fully facing her. "Tori—" He pulled his lips together in a tight line, and she knew. The chilly, disconnected expression testified that he'd come to end their relationship. Their engagement was over.

Her heart dropped to the floor. Her stomach flipped, and nausea hit with a vengeance. "No!" The anguished word slipped out before she could stop it. Tears blurred Spense's image. She slapped her hand across her mouth, attempting to quiet the sobs.

Spense hung his head. "I'm sorry. I just don't have the feelings I once did."

"But"—she glanced down at the diamond ring gracing her left hand—"we're supposed to get married this summer."

He bit his bottom lip, and for the first time that night, his gaze met hers. "I can't. I don't love you anymore." He ran a hand through his raven black hair. "Maybe I never did."

His words had the same effect as a knife slicing through her heart. And the gaping wound bled into her soul. She raised her chin. The tears ran down her cheeks and dripped onto her shirt. "Three years and maybe you never loved me? How can you even say that? What about all the tender e-mails declaring your love? And your assurance that a long-distance relationship would work? What about flying me to Italy last July to propose under the Tuscan sun? The gifts. The flowers. Are you telling me they were all meaningless?" Then it hit her. They'd all stopped sometime last fall.

"I'm sorry. At one time I thought I did." He shook his head. His eyes were icy, the look he'd once carried for her gone.

By the set of his whisker-shadowed jaw, she knew he'd decided. She had no say in her own destiny. Spense King was done with her—with them. "I think you need to leave."

He moved toward her and the door, stopping a couple of feet back. He held out his cupped hand. "May I have the ring?"

She couldn't get it off fast enough. Once it was freed from her finger, she debated throwing it at him. In the end, however, she held it out between her thumb and index finger, returning the precious stone with dignity.

He hesitated then reached for it. Opening the door, she moved aside. He passed through without glancing her way. Ignoring the desire to slam it shut, she pushed it until a quiet click verified it was closed, verified they were finished, done, over. She slid to the floor and lay in a crumpled heap on the taupe carpet, crying until the tears ran dry. Finally after midnight, she picked herself up off the floor and fell across her bed in an exhausted heap of anguish.

one

Valentine's Day

Six weeks passed and not a word from Spense. Tori begged God to change his heart, but to no avail. How did he walk away without a backward glance? She wished she had the same experience with apparently no regret or pain.

Every morning since the breakup, she rose and declared her life a tear-free zone, but of their own accord, a fresh batch showed up sometime during the day. And today proved worse than usual. Today, the day for lovers, was her hardest since the first week. Thank heaven evening neared and so did the end of this rotten weekend.

Normally she and her best friend would go out to some sappy movie, but Jen was teaching in Italy this year. How she missed her. They e-mailed often, but of all years, this was the year Tori needed her the most and had her the least.

She grabbed her purse, heading to her parents' home for the weekly family dinner. Her mom, dad, and Roni were all worried about her, so she dared not miss it, or the whole fam' would land on her doorstep, asking a million questions about how she was feeling, if she was moving on, and how her quiet times were going. She knew they loved her, but since Spense dumped her, she had felt like a bug under a magnifying glass in their presence.

She turned onto her parents' street. *Oh great, Tom and Roni are here.* Part of her wanted to drive by and ignore tonight's dinner, but she dutifully pulled into the driveway, parking behind Tom's expensive little sports car. Her heart crumpled thinking of the two of them so smitten. *I'd hoped they'd be off at some restaurant making goo-goo eyes without me having to witness.*

As she attempted to fall out of love, her twin seemed to be falling right into it for the very first time. Though she wanted to be happy for her sister, she struggled with feelings of jealousy. This was supposed to be her year, not Roni's. Every year was Roni's year.

Plastering a smile on her face, Tori entered through the garage and straight into the kitchen. Roni was in Tom's arms near the sink. Tori paused a moment in the open doorway. Her heart constricted in pain. She took a deep breath, hoping to calm her overcharged emotions. She focused her gaze on the hickory cabinets lining her mom's kitchen instead of the embracing couple.

"Hey." She tried for normal, but the one word sounded shrill. *So glad to see you two lovebirds are at it again.*

They broke apart, ending the intimate scene.

"Tori!" Roni rushed toward her, hugged her, and pulled her into the kitchen, shutting the door on the crisp February air coming from the garage. "How are you?" Her twin, the identical replica of herself, leaned in, inspecting her closely.

How do you think I am? she longed to ask, but instead raised her chin a fraction. "I'm fine. You?"

What a liar she was. Not even her voice sounded fine.

"You sure?" Roni tilted her head to one side, scrutinizing Tori. "Have you been crying?" She voiced her concern in a mere whisper.

"Not in the past couple of hours." Tori couldn't help the flippant reply as she walked around her sister toward the living room. "Where are Mom and Dad?"

"Tor, you've got to get past heartbreak and move on."

She spun around to face Roni. Tom had disappeared during their hug, so it was only the two of them in the kitchen. "That's you, Roni. You flit from guy to guy, barely taking time to breathe before moving on. For me, there has only ever been Spense. You have no idea how it feels to lose the love of your life."

Remorse settled into Roni's expression. "You're right." Her sister strolled across the kitchen toward her. "Let's face it, my longest relationship has been what—six months? I just hate seeing you like this, knowing you go home alone every day and probably cry yourself to sleep each night." She grabbed Tori's hand and squeezed.

"At least I'm not repressing my emotions." Tori hoped to lighten the mood with her half-witted humor.

"Leave it to you to try and be funny." Roni shook her head but smiled at Tori's lame excuse for a joke.

"Well, I'm crying less," Tori admitted. "But how does one move on quickly when her lifelong dream to be a wife and mother vanished on a red-eye to Minneapolis, along with the ring and any hope for a future with the man I've loved since freshman year of college?"

Roni pulled her into another hug. "I'm sorry."

Tori heard the "but" even though Roni never uttered the word, so she said it for her. "But?"

Roni hesitated, and Tori knew she struggled with whether to be the big sister and give advice or keep her mouth shut. "Get out there." The big sister won out. "Meet some nice Christians. Have some fun."

"At my age how will I ever meet another eligible guy? I'm not the outgoing partygoer you are." Tori shook her head.

"The few men who work at my school are married or old. There is nobody at church. Where else do I go?"

"At your age? Need I remind you, dear sister, you are twenty-five, not eighty. And is God incapable of dropping a man on the doorstep of your apartment if He so chooses?"

She ignored the faith question. Hers was weak. God did miracles for Roni, but rarely for her. "I read that after college, the chances of meeting a Mr. Right drop by some huge percentage."

"But that article doesn't factor in God or a sister, for that matter. So in light of that article and your odds, I hope you'll understand tonight's dinner guest."

Mortified, Tori's jaw dropped. "You didn't."

"It's for your own good." She grabbed Tori's arm, dragging her toward the living room.

Anger swept through Tori. Her sister could be so bossy and controlling and pushy. Always trying to run her life.

As soon as they entered the room, Tori spotted the poor, unsuspecting man. His reddish brown hair was buzzed close to his head and his ears stuck out slightly—not like Dumbo, but certainly more than average. He smiled when they entered, and Tori longed for the comfort and familiarity of Spense all the more.

"Colin, this is my sister, Tori." Roni guided her toward the man she was doomed to spend Valentine's Day with. "Tori, one of Tom's roommates, Colin."

Great, he has more than one.

"Nice to meet you, Tori." He took her hand, holding it in his clammy one a bit too long, and shaking it with an overabundance of enthusiasm. "And don't forget usher. Tom's roommate and usher." His gaze rested on Roni.

Usher? Tori glanced at Roni, who was now the one looking mortified.

"Will you be the maid of honor?" Colin's innocent question felt like a blow to her midsection. Surely he was wrong. They barely knew each other. Her gaze bounced from Roni to Tom and back to Roni's ring finger where a large diamond resided. Tom moved the few steps to Roni's side, wrapping a protective arm around her waist. Both of their expressions held apology.

"You're getting married?" Tori said the words in an emotionless monotone, but inside a million feelings churned her stomach until it was upside down and inside out.

Roni gave one brief nod. Her eyes begged for forgiveness.

Hurt ricocheted through every cell in Tori's body. "When were you going to tell me?"

"Sounds like I let the cat out of the bag. I'm sorry." Colin shook his head. Regret lined his face.

"That you did." Tom nodded. "You girls need some time. Colin and I will leave now so you can talk." Tom kissed Roni's cheek and motioned with his head for his roommate to follow. The door closed behind them.

Roni grabbed Tori's hand, pulling her to the large sectional facing the fireplace and TV. Tori picked up one of the red accent pillows and laid it across her lap.

"I'm sorry. I should have told you sooner. He just gave me the ring this morning, but we've been talking about it for a few weeks." Roni's eyes pleaded with Tori to understand. "I was trying to protect you."

"Protect me from what?" Tori rose and paced to the back door. The sunny and clear blue sky belied the sixty-four-degree temperature in Arizona. Truly, it should be rainy and overcast like her soul. Roni was getting married. The wedding her parents announced in the Christmas letter wouldn't be Tori's after all.

Her sister stood next to her as they gazed out over the backyard.

"You were hurting so badly. How could I tell you?"

"No wonder you wanted to rush my getting over Spense." Tori sucked in a deep breath. "So when is the big day?"

"April third."

"April third! That's less than two months away."

"I know." Roni's eyes had a distant, dreamy look. "Will you be my maid of honor?"

"Of course I will." She hugged her sister, praying for the strength to get through the next few weeks. "But are you sure? You just met him on New Year's Day. You barely know him. What do Mom and Dad think?"

"I do know him." Roni's brows rose and crinkled her forehead. "It will be three months and two days when we walk down the aisle. Sounds crazy, doesn't it? But I've never been more sure about anything. He's the one. I'm certain of it. Mom and Dad wish we'd slow down, but we just want to be together."

I hope you're right that he's the one. Much more cautious in nature, Tori came up with dozens of reasons why waiting might be a better idea. But she voiced none of them. In light of all that had transpired this year, Roni might perceive her protests as selfish rather than sincere concern.

"I have to tell you one more thing. This will be harder to hear."

"Is it about Spense?" Somehow she just knew by Roni's expression.

She nodded her head, grabbed Tori's arm, and led her to a seat at the dining room table.

Tori's heart beat a frantic rhythm as she waited—both wanting and not wanting to hear whatever news Roni had uncovered.

"His sister called me today."

"Steph?"

"Yep."

"I wish she would have called me. I needed closure with his family, but no one ever reached out."

"She wanted to but just had no idea what to say. Also, as family, she has a certain unspoken loyalty to her brother."

Tori tried to understand but honestly didn't. She and Steph weren't great friends, but they did e-mail occasionally.

"So what did she have to say?"

Tori searched Roni's pale blue eyes for answers. Their Norwegian ancestry certainly showed itself in their blond hair, blue eyes, and fair skin.

"Spense is getting married in June."

The air swooshed from Tori's lungs. Suddenly his behavior during the autumn months made perfect sense. He must have been seeing someone else. "He wasted no time."

"No he didn't." Roni clasped Tori's hand. "I'm really sorry."

"You've said that phrase a lot today." Tori's lip quivered, but she didn't want to shed another tear over that two-timing jerk. "Do you know the girl's name?"

Roni nodded. "Bella."

Jealousy twisted Tori's insides into knots. "His ex? That Bella?" She closed her eyes, hoping to shut out the pain.

"Yep. You read her right when you were in Minnesota last summer. After seven years, she was still hot on his trail."

"And she won." Tori rose. "I need to go home." She blinked her eyes at a fast pace, trying to hold the tears at bay. She didn't know which emotion was stronger, the anger or the hurt. She grabbed her purse off the couch and headed for the kitchen. "Will you tell Mom and Dad for me?" Then she paused and faced Roni. "Where are they anyway?" She hadn't seen them since her arrival.

"A Valentine's date." Roni squinted her eyes, looking Tori up and down. "Are you sure you should be alone? I can go with you if you'd like."

Tori shook her head. "I'll be fine." She hugged her twin good-bye. "In all honesty, my emotions are all over the place, but it's part of my reality right now. Why don't you call Tom and try to redeem the night minus the roommate? And thanks but no thanks as far as Colin is concerned. Got it?"

"One roommate off the list."

"All roommates off the list," she hollered just as she closed the kitchen door. Once inside her car, she laid her head on the steering wheel, letting the tears fall. Dabbing her eyes, she started the car.

On the drive home, she found herself wondering if Spense proposed today since it was Valentine's Day. Did Bella wear the ring she once wore? How did this happen? She should have moved to Minneapolis instead of staying in Arizona to plan the wedding. That decision cost her everything.

When Tori got to her apartment, she pulled out her new journal from the bookshelf in her bedroom. She'd not written in it at all this year, hoping Spense would wake up one morning and realize he'd made a huge mistake. Hoping they could both forget and move on together. Somehow, not recording their breakup in ink left room for hope, but that obviously would never happen now that he was engaged to someone else. Time to face reality.

In writing, she found release and even healing. *May that be so tonight, Lord. Heal my gaping wounds.* She opened the new leather-bound book filled with blank lines and endless possibility, so like the first day of this year until Spense showed up on her doorstep. Holding the journal near her face, she inhaled the scent of leather and paper. Grabbing her favorite pen from the top desk drawer and a box of Kleenex from the nightstand, she curled up in her preferred corner of the couch and put pen to paper.

On January first when this year began, I would have told you I headed into the best 365 days ever. This twelve-month period should have been filled with wedding planning, bridal showers, an exotic honeymoon. I should have been not only a bride but also a wife and a woman living out her childhood dream, not a woman with a shattered heart.

But instead, the wedding invitation being mailed in the next week or two will read Mr. & Mrs. Ronald V. Wade request the honor of your presence at the wedding ceremony uniting their daughter Veronica Anne to Mr. Thomas Nelson Jr., son of Mr. & Mrs. Thomas Nelson Sr. My name— Victoria Beth Wade—will be nowhere in sight, nor will Spenser King's, my ex-fiancé.

Don't get me wrong—I love Roni. She and I are the best of friends and occasionally the worst of enemies. It's been that way since I exited my mother's womb four minutes and twenty-five seconds after she did. Veronica Anne—Baby A as the doctors called her—has always managed to upstage me at everything in life. Getting married was the one and only thing I would have done first.

I know I sound competitive, and I'm really not. I gracefully accepted that Roni was second in our senior class—I was fifth. She could always outrun me in the mile by several seconds. She's the firstborn. Roni Wade—senior class president, prom queen, the outgoing extrovert. Tori Wade—quiet, introverted, and always in Roni's shadow. And frankly, I lingered comfortably in that shadow, quite content out of the limelight.

But seven months ago, when Spense slipped that diamond on my finger and we headed toward "I do," I found secret pleasure in knowing I'd at last beat Roni at something. I'd win the race to the altar.

Is God punishing me for that prideful attitude? Is that why this has happened?

A few months after my visit with Spense last summer, he became distant. His calls and e-mails nearly stopped. He blamed the new anchor job for a big station in the twin cities, which he started a month after our trip to Tuscany to help Jen move. I never guessed he'd propose while we were there. He'd acted like the trip was a burden.

He used to joke that he was a man from the Twin Cities destined to marry a twin. Yeah right. Six weeks ago, he broke our engagement. Wasn't sure if he ever even loved me. How those words hurt! After all, we'd hung out in the same crowd our first three years of college and started dating our senior year. All together, I've invested six and a half years in a man who is marrying his ex.

On the very same day Spense broke my heart, my sister meets the man of her dreams and in a whirlwind relationship says yes to his proposal on this very day— Valentine's. In only six weeks' time, she says yes. Imagine that! I personally think she's crazy. She may know she loves the guy, but she can't possibly know him yet. They are in for a tough first year.

So now there are two weddings scheduled this year—Roni's and Spense's. Yes, Spense. He's getting married—just not to me. He's marrying his old girlfriend, the one he broke it off with his freshman year of college. He said he'd left his small farm-town life behind and he'd not be returning to her or the *farm. But she moved to the same big city before the signature on his apartment lease had time to dry.*

So my best 365 days have turned into the worst year of my life so far. How will I manage to get through Roni's wedding in a few weeks, Spense's June wedding, or my own cancelled wedding in July?

Tori raised her chin a fraction, grabbed another Kleenex and dabbed her eyes dry, then returned to her writing.

I can do this. I know I can. After all, I can do all things through Christ who gives me strength. At least that's what every well-meaning soul on the face of planet earth keeps reminding me. That and all things work together for good to those who love the Lord. Sometimes I just wish people would give me a silent hug and keep their well-meant platitudes to themselves.

And by the way, I know I sound whiny. Thanks, dear journal, for giving me the freedom to be pathetic. I promise to get over myself soon. With God's help of course. I'll never make it without You, Lord.

two

Wedding Week

Jake Matthews grabbed his bag from the overhead bin and glanced out the plane's window while waiting in the aisle to disembark. He never got over how small-town the Tucson airport was. The population, including the outlying areas, was about a million people, but more of them must ride horses rather than fly because the airport was tiny in comparison to the number of inhabitants.

His cousin Tom's future sister-in-law would pick Jake up here at the airport and drop him off at the tux shop for measurements. *She's recently been dumped, so be nice to her.* Tom's words echoed through his memory. He knew "be nice to her" really meant show an interest, but he'd reminded Tom, *Sorry dude, but you know games aren't my bag. Don't worry, though. I'm always a nice guy. Every grandma on earth wants to fix me up with some sweet girl she knows.*

He'd seen a few pictures of Tom and Roni, so he shouldn't have much trouble spotting her twin. Roni was a little over the top for his taste, but quite attractive nonetheless.

Finally, the line started to move. He lowered his suitcase to its wheels and led it through the tunnel and into the airport. He took the escalator to baggage claim, though he didn't actually have any checked luggage. His ride wouldn't know that, so she'd probably wait for him there.

His gaze searched the area. He noticed a petite blond

also scanning the crowd. That couldn't be her, though. Not flamboyant enough. He waited ten minutes or so, watching for a blond with a short, chic hairstyle and cutting-edge fashion just like the pictures he'd seen of Roni. And from his job as one of the head managers at Schweitzer's Resort, he knew fashion. He'd been exposed to it for the past five years, and he'd picked up a clue or two.

While waiting, he'd noticed a few things about the petite blond standing across the room. She wore her long hair pulled up and held by one of those claw things. She wore regular jeans—nothing fancy or high dollar and even without holes—a huge trend these days. A pale pink T-shirt and matching flip-flops with a cute heart-shaped face topping the package. Now *she* was much more his type. His cousin was the one with the more cutting-edge taste. He preferred down to earth, real, and without tons of makeup hiding who knows what. Could she be Roni's twin? Staring, he noted similarities.

One way to find out. He pulled his cell phone from his pocket and dialed the number Tom had texted him. A moment later, the blond in jeans and flip-flops dug through her oversized bag and pulled out her cell. She glanced at the screen before opening it. "Hello."

"Are you my ride?" he asked, moving toward her. She grinned at him, and he returned it. Nice. Much nicer than her glamorous sister. Pretty, but simple. Her blond hair, a few shades darker than her twin's, was also much longer. A lot of it spilled out of the top of the clippy-thing.

"Hi, I'm Jake, Tom's cousin." He held out his hand, and she accepted.

"Tori, Roni's sister." Her voice reminded him of silk.

"Thanks for picking me up. I'll have my parents' car once I

get to their house, but Tom said his parents rented a limo to haul us around."

She nodded. "They did, and Tom's right. But it's actually a fifteen-passenger van. They decided a van was more practical and gave us more freedom to come and go on a whim."

"A van, huh? Well whatever works." He followed her toward the exit. "So you're a twin." They passed through electronic doors that swung open automatically.

"I am."

"You don't look as much like your sister as I expected."

"Hair, makeup, clothes all make a big difference. Our faces are identical, though. No one confuses us anymore. I'm the plain one, but in elementary school and junior high, we got mixed up all the time."

Plain, huh? Certainly not by his definition. He followed her to a yellow Volkswagen Beetle. "There are a lot of adjectives to describe you, but I wouldn't put 'plain' on the list."

She opened the trunk, not responding to his comment. The only way he knew she'd heard him was the telltale pink highlighting her fair skin. He slid his suitcase in, realizing she and probably a lot of others sold her short while singing Roni's praises. Nope, nothing plain about her—cute, attractive, petite, great smile, but not plain.

"You travel light." Sliding behind the wheel of the car, she turned the key, and the motor purred to life. "Hard to believe you've got enough for a week crammed into that one carry-on."

He laughed, buckling his seat belt. "A few golf shirts. What more can a man need in Tucson, Arizona?"

His phone beeped. "A text." He flipped it open while Tori paid the parking attendant in the booth as they exited the airport. "The guys are running behind, and I'm starved. Would you mind if we stopped at Mi Nidito for some lunch before you drop me at Katrina's to get measured, or do you have somewhere else you need to be?"

"Mi Nidito? It's a family favorite." She shifted her little Bug into third as they picked up speed heading toward town.

"Me, too. I hit it every time I'm home."

"Home? You're from Tucson?"

"Originally. Until college." He gazed at the Catalina Mountains standing tall, proud, and purple to the north. "Tom and I were like brothers—both the same age and very tight." The sky was as clear and blue as his Idaho skies.

"So, you're twenty-eight?" She glanced in his direction while slowing for a red light.

He nodded.

"Where did you head for college?"

"University of Idaho in Boise offered me a golf scholarship, so I ended up in Idaho, loved it, and stayed."

"Oh."

He laughed at her more-than-typical response when he mentioned his favorite state in the entire nation.

"What?" Her brow furrowed as she pulled away from the traffic light.

"You've never been to Idaho, have you?"

"No, nor is it honestly on my list of dying-to-visit vacation destinations. I mean, people are born there, but don't they grow up and move away?"

He laughed harder. "No—not true. You need to make Idaho your next vacation destination. I promise that you'll fall in love."

She shrugged, but the doubt written across her face said more than mere words could convey. She pulled into the

Mexican restaurant parking lot but had to back out and try the south lot. No empty spaces there either. They finally parked across Fourth Avenue in another restaurant's empty back lot.

"I always feel so bad for this place."

"Yeah, nobody in Tucson competes with Mi Nidito, but it must be double the insult to provide parking to their overflow of customers."

"Especially when you always have so few."

Tori waited on the bench under the covered porch while he went in and put their names on the waiting list. The smells of spicy food floated around, and his stomach rumbled.

"Twenty minutes," he informed her when he rejoined her outside.

"Not bad. Some days are an hour or more." She pushed her bangs to the side.

"Believe me, I've waited that long more than once here. I won't do that for many places, but you either wait or miss the best tacos in the world."

"For me it's the cheese enchiladas." When she grinned, a little dimple in her cheek barely made itself visible. "Do you come here every time you're back in town?"

"At least twice. Once coming in from the airport and then on my way back to the airport. But I try to fit in a couple of extra visits, if I have time. Speaking of airport, could you— would you be my ride? I fly out very early Monday morning. How do you feel about O-dark thirty?"

"I'd be happy to give you a ride, especially early. I have to be at work by eight."

"You sure you don't mind?"

She shook her head.

"I'm staying at my parents' house, but they're on a month-long European vacation. They hated to miss the wedding, but had saved for this many years. They'd just finalized their plans when Tom hit them with an impending wedding date. Too many of their tickets were nonrefundable, so they opted to go."

"I don't blame them. When you only give people six weeks, you're bound to lose a few." She shrugged, and he sensed animosity toward Tom and Roni's fast-paced plans.

He changed the subject, not wanting to spout his reservations to Roni's sister—after all, she might not see this marriage as impulsive and idiotic as he did. He'd tried to talk to Tom, but he and Roni were determined. "So where do you work?"

"I'm a high school teacher. Basic accounting."

"Accounting. . .so you have the summer off?" His brain was running ahead to Allison's two-month maternity leave.

"Yes." Her voice and mood changed with his question.

"Matthews, party of two," blasted over the loudspeaker.

They rose from the bench, and he held the door open for Tori. They followed the waitress to their booth along the side wall.

He eyed the bright, festive, oversized flowers. "This place never changes." Jake took his menu but laid it aside, already knowing what he planned to order. Tori did the same.

"So, it's Monday, and you're here, not at school." His eyes roamed over the bright potted plants, Mexican tile, and bright Mexico décor.

"Luckily I'm on spring break—otherwise this wedding week would prove difficult. Roni planned a full schedule."

The waitress breezed by, stopping to take their order. She grabbed the menus and disappeared.

"I like the way they are doing this prewedding week. Lots of activities and time to spend together."

"Roni hates that so often your closest friends fly in, hit the rehearsal dinner, attend the wedding, and fly out. She didn't want it to feel rushed. Of course, not everyone can come for the whole week."

"I'm glad I could. And you, too, for that matter." He winked at the cute blond seated across from him and found himself looking forward to spending time getting to know Tori better. Who knew, but maybe by the end of the week he'd convince her to come to Idaho and work for him this summer. He needed an accounts payable clerk for Allison's two-month maternity leave, and since Tori taught basic accounting, she just might fit the resort's needs. And his. . .

Whoa, they'd just met. That thought came out of nowhere. He'd not dated since Kate, and that was a few years ago. He'd let her seal his fate as a bachelor. Man, had he misread their relationship.

ને

The waitress set their hot plates in front of them. Tori picked up her napkin.

"Would you like me to pray?" Ernest brown eyes fixed on her.

"That would be nice." She bowed her head while Jake gave thanks. His offer surprised her. Spense hated praying in public—made him feel like a spectacle. Rich irony since he was a local celeb up in his land of a thousand lakes.

"Amen." She unfolded her napkin, placing it across her jean-clad legs.

"So, I was thinking"—he wore a mischievous grin—"how about a trade? One taco for one enchilada?"

"Deal." She pushed her plate toward him.

She studied him while he was preoccupied with the food.

His light brown hair was kissed with gold, and his hazel eyes danced when he talked. Not nearly as striking as Spense, he was more ruggedly attractive where Spense was downright handsome. Spense was suits, ties, and designer clothes. Her guess was Jake spent more time in jeans or shorts. Like today, he wore khaki cargo shorts and a striped, collared, short-sleeve knit shirt in shades of greens and browns.

He made the transaction and pushed her plate back across the table. Biting into his taco, he said, "I think these tacos will be in heaven." He smiled up at her, and deep dimples creased his cheeks.

She laughed. After months of wearing a cloak of grief, Tori felt lighter today than she had since the breakup. "Time heals all wounds" sounded like a platitude, but with the passing of weeks and then months, the ache really had lessened.

She had foolishly ventured onto Spense's Facebook page a couple of weeks ago, and seeing photos of him and Bella reopened the wound a bit. His status was still engaged, just a different girl by his side.

"Hey, where'd you go?"

Jake's question brought her focus back to the here and now. "Huh?"

"Is it the food, the company, or something else?" Sincere eyes searched her face.

"Definitely not the food." She'd divert his inquiry with a touch of humor.

"Hopefully not the company." His raised brow challenged her to tread carefully.

She scratched her head. "Hmm?" After a long pause, she added, "Probably not the company."

"Just a probably, huh? The food was a definitely." He adopted a sad puppy-dog face.

Giggling, she laid down her fork. "Sorry, my mind wandered. Nothing to do with the company."

"Whew. I was worried I'd been demoted from average guy to downright boring."

How about charming? And certainly not average. "Nope."

"So what's on our agenda this week? I think I left my itinerary on my kitchen table."

"Don't worry, Roni has spares. She's super organized and super efficient."

He chuckled. "Good news for me."

"Today is the fittings for the guys and tonight a barbecue at my parents'. Tomorrow is a trip to Mount Lemmon. Wednesday, a hike in Sabino Canyon. Thursday is the Desert Museum. Friday, golf for the guys with mani's and pedi's for us and a bridesmaids' tea. I know it sounds touristy, but as Roni says, it's stuff most of us never do. And fun things to do as a group.

"Late Friday afternoon is the rehearsal and then rehearsal dinner. And Saturday is the big day. Sunday is brunch at my parents' followed by gift opening. Roni and Tom have to be at the airport at five to catch their flight to Florida. Early Monday they fly to Jamaica. You leave, and I return to high school."

"Wow. It's a full week. If one wished to, could one skip, say, the Desert Museum for a game of golf?" He pushed his empty plate toward the middle of the table.

"Only if one is willing to risk the wrath of Roni." She took her last bite of enchilada, savoring the flavor of the sauce.

"Wrath?" His expression grew serious.

She nodded.

"So attendance is required?"

"Sorry to say it is."

"So you'll be there?"

"Most certainly. And so will you. As the best man and maid of honor, we are expected to set an example." She used her schoolteacher voice to emphasize the importance of attendance at all events.

"I see."

The waitress dropped off their bill and carried off their empty plates.

"I'm sorry, we should have asked for separate checks." Tori dug her wallet out of her purse. "I have a twenty."

"Not on your life." He snatched up the check. "First of all, you picked me up at the airport, so treating you to lunch is a given. But second, when a man and a lady dine together, the man pays. It's the right thing to do. Now if you'll excuse me." He rose, taking the check with him up to the cash register.

Tori kind of liked his point of view. Many women would consider him a Neanderthal, but she liked men who opened doors and treated women as the fairer sex that God created them to be. Yep, Jake had some appealing qualities, not that she was interested.

Tori took Jake to Katrina's, the shop that sold wedding gowns and rented tuxes all in one location. "I guess I'll see you tonight then at the barbecue."

"That you will." She sent him a smile.

He climbed out of her little car, bent over, and added, "Tori, it was really nice meeting you."

"Ditto."

"You'll make the Desert Museum bearable for the fortieth time in my life." He winked and shut the door.

She wore a silly grin all the way to the beauty shop for the trial run. It was nice to focus on something besides her pathetic life. But it was hard to forget that this week she'd planned to dedicate her time off for her own nuptial planning, not for her sister's wedding. The thought brought a sharp pang to her heart. She took a deep breath, raised her chin, and headed into the shop. *I've got to keep taking captive my thoughts and not let the what-ifs run away with me.*

"Hey, girls," Tori greeted Roni, Tom's sisters Marti and Kristi, Roni's best friend Renee, and Roni's college roommate Ariel all with hugs.

"Great, everyone's here. Right on time. Let's get started." Roni led them into the Gadabout Salon, where they'd all have their hair done— a practice run for the big day. On her teaching salary, Tori couldn't normally afford this place, so for her, the high-dollar salon was a treat.

Her sister and Tom were sparing no expense on this wedding. Roni was a lawyer, and Tom was in pharmaceutical sales, so they had the money to dole out. Her wedding would have been much simpler, cheaper, less ostentatious.

There it was again. The cancelled wedding insisted on raising its ugly head, even though Tori would love to quit remembering.

"Did you pick Jakey up and get him delivered to Tom?"

"Jakey?" Tori laughed. "Sounds like we're talking about a four-year-old."

"That's what we all call him," Kristi concurred. She looked into a mirror, pulling her dark hair into an upsweep.

"Jakey, Tommy, Marti, and Kristi." Marti tried to pull her shorter, lighter hair back, but to no avail. "He was more like our brother than our cousin. We were all close."

"Was he an only child?" For some reason that thought surprised her.

"He was." Marti turned to Roni. "I don't think my hair will go up."

"They are miracle workers here, but if not, they'll do something sophisticated." Roni pulled a lock of Marti's hair away from her head as if measuring it. "So did you like him?" She turned her gaze on Tori.

"Of course." Tori knew Roni meant like him with a capital *L*. "What's not to like? He's nice, polite. Jakey was even well-behaved." She made the statement in her best teacher voice.

Tori did like Jake—a lot—and found herself curious about him, but that was not information she'd share with her pushy, life-planning twin. However, she'd love to engage Tom's sister in conversation and learn more about this interesting cousin of theirs.

three

As soon as Jake arrived at the Wade home for the barbecue, he searched for Tori, using the excuse that she was the only familiar face, except his cousins of course. He found her in the kitchen at the sink. Her hair was swept up, leaving an ivory neck exposed, and he couldn't help staring. He imagined himself waltzing up behind her and placing a tender kiss on that graceful neck of hers. Finally, he tore his gaze away, knowing full well that long-distance romances never worked. But something about her appealed to him. Something about her made him almost brave enough to want to try it again.

He cleared his throat. "There you are."

She turned and smiled, wiping damp hands on a red dish towel. "Hi, Jake."

"I was looking for that one familiar face in a river of strangers. Can I give you a hand?"

"Sure. I'm washing the veggies for the salad. How trustworthy are you with a knife, Jakey?"

He rolled his eyes. "Who's guilty, Marti or Kristi?"

"Both." She pulled her lips tightly together, but he could see the laughter bubbling just below the surface.

"Glad you're amused."

The giggles came unrestrained. Her eyes sparkled and he joined her, finding her laughter infectious and fun.

"You don't mind if I call you that, do you, Jakey?"

"You might as well. Everyone else in Tucson does." He

33

joined her at the sink and started chopping fresh vegetables. She talked about the high school where she taught and shared some funny student stories. She kept him laughing all the way through the salad-making.

"Hey, you two about done?" Colin came up behind them. He placed a hand on Tori's shoulder and one on Jake's. "We're going to play horseshoes with boy/girl teams. Tori, since you still owe me a date, I thought we might pair up."

Jake glanced at Tori, wondering if she and Colin might have something brewing. Nope. One look at her pleading expression clued him in. He turned, nonchalantly removing Colin's hand from his shoulder. "Sorry, she's already taken."

Colin shrugged. "Great, that leaves me with one of Tom's sisters." He headed back into the great room. "Hey, Kristi," they heard him call.

"Thanks. I owe you."

&

"If you don't mind my asking, why does he believe you owe him a date? You're clearly not interested." His eyes searched hers for the answer.

"Long story, but my well-meaning, pain-in-the-patooty sister has set me up with every single one of Tom's roommates—all four of them."

"Seriously?" He finished washing his hands at the kitchen sink, and she tossed him a clean dish towel.

"Seriously." Then she filled him in on the Valentine's date that never happened, only saying that something came up. Admitting a meltdown over her twin's impending nuptials made her sound shallow to the max, so she left that detail unsaid.

"So you've been out with every one of Tom's roommates and still owe Colin his night on the town? I hadn't pegged you as such a player," he teased.

"Oh yeah, that's me. Out every weekend with a different guy."

"Well, since you chose me over Colin, let's go out there and kick it. I hope you're good because I'm competitive."

"Lucky for you, I'm decent. Dad loves horseshoes, so I grew up playing. I can hold my own against everyone but Roni." *No surprise there.*

"Well, lucky for you, I beat my cousin at anything and everything, so that evens the odds."

Sure enough, as the contest progressed, the final two pairs were Roni and Tom versus Jake and Tori.

After several close games and the score tied, she hit a leaner for the win. Jake grabbed her and swung her around. He did like to win! When he lowered her feet to the ground, he raised her hand high in the air holding his. "It was a hard-fought victory, but in the end the team of Jake and Tori claimed the win with a stunning finish by Tori Wade." Then he and Tori took a bow.

Everyone laughed and applauded.

"Now if you'll excuse us, we're starving." Still holding her hand, he led her over to the buffet tables her mom had just finished setting up. "After the bride and groom, of course." He held out his hand to encourage them to take the lead.

After everyone left that evening, Tori and her mom worked in the kitchen, cleaning up. "Another successful party, Mom. The food was great."

"Thanks, honey. That Jake seems like a nice man."

She smiled, wondering when someone would misinterpret tonight and couple them together. "He is a great guy, but not really my type, so don't go getting any big ideas."

Her mom laughed. "Got it. But it's too bad because he'll

make some girl a fine catch one day."

Yes, he will. But her heart and mind were too full of Spense to even consider another man. According to one book she read, it would take her at least three years to recover—half the length of their relationship. And she'd had a crush on him starting freshman year, long before he knew she existed. And she'd still be hurting, long after he'd forgotten.

ﬞ

"Mount Lemmon. I haven't been there since junior high or early high school." Jake grabbed her hand and pulled her into the seat next to him. Then he leaned in close to her ear. "Just protecting you from the roommates." He enjoyed that role. Face it, he enjoyed her.

"Thanks." She gave his hand a squeeze before pulling hers loose. His heart beat a little faster when she was near. "Every damsel in distress needs a hero."

"So I'm your hero?" He liked the sound of that.

"Time will tell." She raised a perfect brow. "Can you keep me safe on the ski lift and away from those unappealing men?"

"I can do as madam wishes." He kissed her hand, enjoying their playful banter. "I shan't leave your side this day."

Tori cracked up. Man was she beautiful when she laughed. The most refreshing thing about her was how unaware she was of her beauty, grace, and charm. Sadly, he was much too aware. And in less than a week, he'd have to tell her good-bye.

"This was a great idea to rent a fifteen-passenger van." Jake opted to change the conversation to get his mind off Tori and all her attributes. "Much better than a limo."

"Yeah. They thought of everything." Tori gazed out the window, seemingly deep in thought. Something troubled her. Must be that recent breakup Tom told him about. Another reason to steer clear. He didn't need to be her rebound guy.

Ron, Tori's dad, led them in a rendition of one hundred bottles of coke on the wall. The singing and goofiness pulled Tori out of her sadness. Soon she was singing and smiling with the rest of them.

True to his word, he kept the other men at bay. They spent the day together, and he couldn't remember ever enjoying another woman more, not even Kate. She was way too high maintenance. Jake fell asleep that night feeling as content as a well-fed pup.

The next morning they headed to Sabino Canyon for more hiking, a little cliff diving, and a tram ride to the top. Once they were at the top, people broke into smaller groups and chose different trails. He and Tori ended up alone on the trail to Seven Falls. They were the only ones heading that direction.

Today she'd french braided her hair, and he found himself wanting to tug on it. She looked cute in her shorts, hiking boots, and backpack.

They'd walked about a half mile or so in silence. He decided to broach the subject she'd left unsaid—her breakup. He knew from his own past experience that she'd heal quicker by talking about it. "I love the desert. The cactus, the wildlife, all of it. Idaho holds my heart in many ways, but there is no place like home."

"So many people see the desert as barren wasteland, but it is so glorious. It's sad that the beauty is often missed."

She could have been describing herself. In the last twenty-four hours, he'd realized Tori was often overlooked because Roni's presence overpowered hers. Yet to him, she was the beautiful one, the kind one, the tender one.

Lord, how do I bring up the breakup? He had no idea what

to say, so he just jumped in. "Tom tells me that you recently faced a tough breakup." He was following her up the trail, so he had no way of seeing the emotions in her expression.

"I wondered if you knew." She paused and faced him. "Is that why you're being so nice to me?"

He shook his head. "I'm a sucker for a beautiful woman."

Pink tinted her cheeks, and she lowered her gaze.

"Seriously, I've been right where you are—gaping wound in my heart. I found some healing and freedom once I opened up to someone and spilled my guts. My someone was an older woman at work who I barely knew. Sometimes it's easier with a mere acquaintance than someone closer. I'll be your someone. . .if you'd like."

She raised her gaze to meet his. "Thanks, Jake. How do you feel about crying women and tear-soaked shirts?"

He smiled. Her wit appealed to him.

"Crying women I can handle, unless I'm the one who made them cry. In your case, I'll be safe. Shirts wash."

She turned and continued heading up the trail to the top of the cactus-strewn hill. He wasn't sure if she'd take him up on it or not. But he'd offered. *I'll be your someone, if you'd like.* Those words meant a lot more than he'd intended. A whole lot more.

≈

Tori weighed his offer. She arrived at the crest of the hill slightly breathless. Placing her hand above her eyes to shade them from the blazing sun, she gazed out over the valley where Tucson sat. Surrounded by mountains on all sides, the city had spread as far as it could in every direction, even up into the foothills.

She glanced at Jake. He studied her. Not sure she could put a voice to her breakup one more time, she asked him,

"Will you tell me your story?"

"Sure."

So as they started up the trailhead marked Seven Falls, he began. "I met Kate shortly after taking the job on Schweitzer Mountain. She worked at the front desk and had just finished her degree in hotel management. I should have known I was just a passing fancy, as was the job, until something better came along."

She continued to lead the way down the narrow trail—mountain to her right and cliff to her left, wondering what Kate looked like and if she'd loved Jake. Seemed he'd be an easy man to love.

"I'd just graduated as well with a major in business and minor in accounting. I, too, worked the front desk, but planned to stick around and work my way up the ladder. Not Kate, she had no time for ladders." Tori heard him drink some water from his water bottle.

She took the break to ask, "Was Kate pretty?"

"Yeah. Yeah she was." His tone had a smile to it.

"What did she look like?" She wondered what his type was.

"Tall, brunette, with these gorgeous green eyes."

I'm so not his type. That's a relief—I think.

"When she flirted with me, her eyes sent off sparks like the Fourth of July. But she didn't want me, at least not forever, and I'm loyal to a fault—a forever kind of guy."

"A forever kind of guy. That's poetic. What girl wouldn't want you?" *Except me of course. Bad timing and all.*

"Well, not Kate. She changes guys and jobs on a regular basis. And always manages to move up in both realms. Last I heard, she was dating a professional baseball player."

"That's impressive. She must be pretty because everyone

I've seen on TV linked to an athlete always looks like a model or movie star."

He shrugged. "Now I wonder what she ever saw in me."

"I wonder the same thing!" She shook her head at how similar their stories were.

"Gee, thanks."

"Not about you. About Spense and I." The narrow trail widened a bit, and Tori waited for him to come alongside her. She stayed near the mountain. He could walk cliff-side.

"Spense is the guy?"

She nodded, keeping her gaze straight ahead, not wanting Jake to see the pain she fought to hide. "Were you and Kate engaged?"

"I'd bought the ring and planned the proposal so it was romantic enough to hit the Hallmark channel, but she never knew."

"Maybe she'd have stayed, Jake. I think you should have told her."

He shook his head. "Kate was intentional. Her life followed a well-thought-out plan. She wanted a man of far greater importance than me. And a much higher caliber job than Schweitzer could ever offer."

"But—"

"I asked her what could make her stay. She looked at me with frosty eyes and said nothing, absolutely nothing. She was headed for San Francisco, but suggested we could try a long-distance relationship. Maybe if things worked out, I could move there in a year or two. So she kept me dangling. Backup man number one. Come to find out, she also had a new boyfriend that she'd met at the new job."

"Was she a Christian?" That sort of behavior appalled Tori's rather naive side.

"Said she was. We went to church together, but not a lot of depth. I should have seen it, but chose not to."

They reached the end of the trail. Tori settled onto a log, dropping her backpack on the ground next to her. "I'm sorry. How long were you together?"

He joined her on the log. "A year in Sandpoint and another year of texts, e-mails, and late-night phone calls."

"Sounds like you liked her a lot." Tori unzipped her backpack, pulling out her lunch, and Jake did the same.

"I did. Is that what happened with you and Spense?" He unzipped his baggie and removed a sandwich.

"Not at first, but by the end. At the breakup scene—which felt very much like a crime scene—he said he might not have ever loved me." She opened a power bar. "I hate that! Do you hate that? It's so cruel."

"Truth is, it's the way he absolved himself of guilt. 'I'm doing you a favor because come to find out, my feelings for you weren't real anyway.'" He bit into his ham and Swiss on rye.

"Exactly. Thank you very much." Tori swatted at a fly.

"I was the one left stunned, and she moved on with nary a backward glance."

"Me, too. So how long ago did this happen? And how long did it take you to heal?"

"It's been five years." He wadded up his baggie, tossing it into his backpack.

"Does it still hurt when you think about it?" She hoped not.

"Yes, but not the way you mean. It hurts to think how stupid I was. What an idiot!"

"And has there been anyone since?"

"Nope. I date occasionally. Dinner with an interesting guest at the resort, but we both know it's going nowhere."

"Have you considered the whole Internet thing? More than one person has wanted to sign me up at one site or another."

He laughed, pulling an apple out of his bag. "Me, too. My mother even went so far as to fill out the form for me. All I had to do was hit SEND. I hit DELETE instead. This will sound corny I'm sure, but I'm waiting for God and His girl."

"Wow." His honesty and his approach impressed her. "What a novel idea. You could be quoting me because I said the exact same thing to my sister. God moves a little too slow for her, though."

He chuckled. "For me sometimes, too, but I keep waiting."

They hiked down to the falls, but it was barely a trickle. "I remember when I was a kid, water poured over those rocks. It was beautiful. Idaho has no shortage of water. As a matter of fact, other than Alaska, she has the most miles of rivers."

"How do your parents feel about you being so far away?"

"They bought a condo up on the mountain and come every summer. If I ever end up married with kids, I think they'd move there."

He searched her face. "Now it's your turn. Tell me about you and Spense."

She felt relaxed and comfortable. He was easy to talk to, so the story she'd protected and kept close to her heart poured out like rain from the sky. She told him the good, the bad, and the embarrassing. She was glad they were walking so she didn't see his face, not wanting to witness disapproval or pity.

"So this wedding is painful for you?"

"I'm embarrassed to say so, but yes. I feel so petty. Hanging out with you has been a nice distraction, though." Shame crept up her spine just admitting it aloud. She was a horrible Christian example.

"I'm glad—after all, I am your hero. But don't feel guilty, Tori. You lost a dream that you carried close to your heart. You're grieving. It's hard to be around happy people when your heart's cracked wide open."

"Yeah, misery does love company, doesn't it?"

"I don't think you want your sister to be miserable, do you?"

"No. But couldn't she be normal and date for a year like everyone else? I'd have had some time to heal. Instead here she is, marrying her perfect match three months and two days after they meet. Everything always works for her. She's the blessed one." But though it looked perfect on the outside, Tori knew in her heart Roni was marrying a virtual stranger, and getting to know a man after she married him wasn't smart. What if it turned out she didn't like him much?

He grabbed her arm and pulled her to a stop. When she turned to face him, he asked, "Tori, do you see yourself as less? Some references you've made about you and Roni made me wonder."

She took her time answering. The question startled her. *Do I?* She recalled some of her labels. *I'm the plain twin. Roni's perfect. Everything works for her.*

" 'Cause if you do, it's a lie. You're beautiful, funny, smart."

As Jake recited her attributes, her heart quickened at his words.

"Tom's roommates are waiting in line for you." He winked.

"Some real catches they are, too." Her words brought conviction. "Great, now I'm being prideful, thinking I deserve better than them."

"Tori, stop beating yourself up. Stop competing with Roni. Be you, because I think you're pretty wonderful." He leaned in, and she thought he might kiss her. Did she want him to? He bypassed her lips and placed a tender kiss on her cheek.

Was she disappointed or relieved? Maybe a little of both.

He lingered near her ear, his warm breath against her neck stirring up more confusion. "Start believing that you really are fearfully and wonderfully made. I know it, and so does God."

four

Jake had no trouble accepting the fact that Tom fell for Roni in three weeks and asked her to marry him three weeks after that. After all, he fell for her sister in three days. Monday he liked her. Tuesday he was enchanted. Wednesday, smitten. And today young tender shoots of deep feelings were pushing their way to the surface. Not quite ready to use the "L" word, he knew he was close.

He barely slept, couldn't stop smiling, and couldn't wait to see her again. "God, is she the one I've been waiting for?" he asked while running the electric razor over his chin and cheeks. "The helpmeet You promised me in Your good and perfect time?"

He wondered how she would have responded if his lips landed on hers yesterday instead of on her cheek. He'd thought about it. Considered it. But when it came right down to it, he'd detoured at the last second.

"Chicken." He spoke to his image in the mirror. "No, I did the right thing. I'll have to take it nice and slow. Tori's nowhere near ready to meet the love of her life." But he felt pretty sure that was the role God created him to play—Tori Wade's adoring husband. Yep, he could do that with pleasure. Now God just needed to tell her.

Tom picked Jake up at his parents' in the *big, big van* as they'd all dubbed it. Next they headed to the Wades' to meet the girls. Upon arriving, he vacated the passenger seat and claimed the very back seat. That way he and Tori had some privacy. The others were starting to notice their connection.

When Tori climbed into the van, her eyes met his for a brief moment, and then she averted them. He spotted indecision and wasn't sure she'd come all the way to the back and sit with him, but she did.

"Desert Museum, here we come." He scooched over, and she settled in next to him.

"I'm about as excited as you are. It's a great place, and I love seeing all the animals of the Southwest in their natural habitat. But as you said Monday, after about the fortieth time, it gets old."

"How about if we start at the restaurant with some coffee? Then we'll decide where to go from there," he said in a conspiratorial whisper.

She smiled. "Good plan."

Once they got there and bought their tickets, Tori and Jake ducked into the gift shop. After everyone else moved on toward the bat exhibit, they slipped into the restaurant unnoticed. Being patient was going to be tough for Jake. He already fought draping his arm around her shoulder or grabbing a hand. What he'd really like to do was stand facing her, touching her velvet-soft face and pouring out his heart. Not a good idea, of that he was certain. She thought Tom and Roni rushed things. . . .

They settled into a booth in the corner. "Jake, I want to thank you so much for yesterday." She bit her bottom lip. "You are—without a doubt—the nicest, sweetest guy that I've met in a long time."

Uh-oh. Nice and sweet always leads to phrases like "I think we'd be great friends" or "I think of you like a brother."

"Thanks for listening yesterday. It really did help to say it out loud."

He smiled and gave her hand a short squeeze, careful to keep it friendly and nothing more. "I know talking it through was cathartic for me when I faced a broken heart, so I'm glad I could be the one to help you."

The waitress came, and they each ordered a cup of coffee. They sat for a couple of hours chatting about life and laughing, but Tori made certain they stayed away from anything personal. When they caught up with the group, she hung more with the other girls than with him, making him doubt his earlier assumptions.

≥

The following morning on her drive to the nail salon, Tori reevaluated her decision to cool things down with Jake. They'd had so much fun the three previous days. And yesterday, hanging out with the girls was a dud in comparison. She just didn't want to give him the wrong idea. He was a great guy— too great. Her heart was nowhere near ready for round two. Honestly, she wondered if she'd ever be.

She parked her Bug next to Roni's red Miata. Roni and Renee were both already there. Roni was at the front desk, and Renee was over at the polish station. Tori joined her there.

Renee picked up a bronze-colored bottle, but after studying it for several seconds, she replaced it. "So, Tori, is there another wedding on the horizon?" Her casual question stabbed at Tori's heart, an unpleasant reminder of her and Spense's breakup.

Tori grabbed a plum shade. "Spense and I broke up, remember?" She walked away without even a glance at Renee.

"Tori, wait."

Tori ignored the plea. Since she was the first one to choose her shade, she made her way to the very last pedicure station.

A small Asian woman welcomed her, took the polish, and started running water into the basin. She turned on Tori's massage chair, which felt good against her sore muscles from the hike two days ago.

Why would Renee be so cruel? Tori wished she knew. *Great, she's heading my direction.*

"Tori, I'm so sorry. My words were careless. I was teasing you about Jake, not even thinking about the emotions my words would evoke."

"Jake?"

"You two seem, well. . .close. We thought twin number two might have a whirlwind romance like twin number one. How cool would that be if twins married cousins?"

Tori couldn't believe what she was hearing. "Jake and I barely know each other and are just friends." A little place in Tori's brain screamed, *Liar!* A different time might yield a harvest, but in this season she couldn't think past the constant ache in her heart.

"Every one of us is thinking you guys are a couple. The way you look at each other—we just assumed."

Tori's face grew warm. "You know what they say about assuming. I don't know what you're seeing, but I promise that we are just friends. And if it were more, which it clearly is not, he lives a long way from here, and I'm done with long-distance relationships."

Renee shrugged. "Okay. Whatever you say." But Tori heard the doubt in her tone. Why couldn't anyone leave her life alone? They were all a bunch of gossips that had no idea what they were talking about. Tori closed her eyes during the pedicure, trying to shut out her annoyance and relax.

છે

Jake stood next to Tom at the front of the church for the

wedding rehearsal, the other groomsmen standing in a line to his left. They hadn't seen the girls all day, so he anticipated Tori's entrance.

Tom leaned over and whispered, "Just tell her how you feel and get it over with."

"What? Who?" He stared at his cousin like he had three heads.

"Tori." Tom gave him that you're-not-fooling-me expression.

"There is nothing between us but a barely budding friendship," Jake assured him. "I've known her less than a week." He couldn't let anyone in on his plan to woo Tori very slowly and carefully. If he admitted it to another soul besides God, soon word would spread, Tori would hear, and she'd bolt. Nope. He'd discuss it with God daily and wait. Waiting wasn't his thing, so God asked it of him often.

"Yeah right. Everybody sees it. Why not admit it?"

Jake shrugged. *Actually, I can. Tori's the problem here.*

The music started—Pachelbel's "Canon in D." The flower girl came into sight first, the church's wedding coordinator right next to the four-year-old, speaking words of encouragement and instruction. Following her was Ariel, then Renee, followed by both his cousins. Finally! Tori came through the double doors. A pale yellow sundress set off her violet blue eyes. Down the aisle she moved gracefully toward them, toward him. His heart jumped into overdrive, and he wondered if anyone could see it through his striped-knit polo.

His eyes never veered far from her the entire practice run. They smiled at each other several times, and with each one, his heart did a little jig. After all the staging and instructions were over, the minister said, "After the pronouncement that you're man and wife and kissing the bride, I'll introduce you, and then you'll leave down the aisle together." He motioned for Tom and Roni to go ahead. Turning to Tori, he said, "You will meet Jake center stage." They did as they were instructed, her arm draping through his.

This was right. This was how it should be. He and Tori arm in arm. Now how was God going to convince her?

❧

The wedding day arrived. Tori waited in the vestibule as the girls in front of her departed through the double doors one at a time. The lilies and roses in her bouquet shook slightly, and she tried to steady her hand. Her mind had been on Spense all morning. She took a deep breath. *Don't go there again. If you do, you'll never make it through this ceremony in one piece.*

She pulled her lips together in a tight line and blinked her eyes, fighting the tears that begged to be set free. The wedding coordinator nodded at her. She raised her chin and forced a wide smile.

Her dad chose that moment to kiss her cheek. Her chin quivered. She stepped through the double doors. A sea of faces fixed their eyes on her. How many knew she should have been the first Wade bride, not Roni?

She looked straight ahead, and her gaze caught Jake's. He sent her a smile, and it gave her strength. She kept her eyes plastered to his face—his expression understanding, knowing, yet encouraging. He, her dad, and Jen were the only ones who seemed to have a clue just how difficult this night was for her. Jen called first thing this morning, and they cried together. Her dad had given her an extra long hug, but everyone else seemed to have forgotten that this was her year.

She made it to the front and climbed the stairs to the stage where the rest of the bridal party stood. As soon as she faced the crowd, her mother stood, and all the guests followed suit. At the sight of her sister on her dad's arm, a tear slid down her cheek.

Roni looked beautiful in her gown of white. It was nothing like the more traditional dress Tori had chosen, but gorgeous nonetheless. How would she get through the ceremony? She glanced at Jake. He smiled and mouthed, "I can do all things through Christ."

Nodding, she focused on the verse, saying it over and over in her head. She shut out everything and everyone. Each time the words echoed through her mind, she felt a little stronger, a little more able.

The wedding ceremony felt surreal. She was there, but not really. In truth, she sensed being wrapped in the arms of Christ as He tenderly ministered to her through this painful time. When the ceremony ended, she met Jake center stage, and they maneuvered the stairs together.

"You doing okay?"

"I am, thanks to you. That verse was just the reminder I needed. I had no idea how much this would hurt. How truly raw I still am."

"I'm not surprised. You've only had a few months to heal."

They nodded and smiled at the crowd as they passed the pews. Tori decided she was with the most eligible man at the wedding. Yep. No doubt about it. He was not a pretty boy like Spense, but a hunk nonetheless. And a thoughtful, tender man.

ॐ

After they finished pictures, the DJ introduced each member of the wedding party. Jake and Tori ran onto the dance floor when they were introduced, waving and smiling. Then they took their places at the head table next to Tom and Roni.

Jake opted to stick to Tori like glue. The hurt she desperately tried to hide lingered just below the surface. He saw it in her eyes, read it in her expression. It made him want to hunt down one Spenser King and give him a piece of his mind or a punch in the face, which was what the jerk deserved.

Who—in his right mind—would leave a girl like Tori? She had it all—brains, beauty, and a sensitive spirit attuned to the Lord. What guy threw that sort of woman away like a piece of garbage? He deserved to be hanged from the nearest tree.

Finally after dozens of conversations, the bride and groom's first dance, and the father-daughter dance, the wedding party took the floor to a slow Celine Dion song. He pulled Tori into his arms. She rested her head against his chest. Could she hear his heart beating a tune just for her?

"My mind keeps wandering to *my* wedding, *my* dress, *my* plans. I feel so selfish and self-absorbed."

"I think what you're feeling is normal. Don't be so hard on yourself."

She stopped moving and looked deep in his eyes. "Thank you, Jake." Her mouth curved upward. "You have been such a great friend this week."

The music stopped. He led her outside onto the balcony. The Santa Catalina Mountains stood majestic in the shadows of the night. A full moon lingered overhead. She shivered. He removed his coat and draped it over her bare shoulders.

She glanced up at him. Tears glistened in her eyes. She fought a valiant battle to keep them at bay.

He shoved his fisted hands deep into the front pockets of his black tux pants, fighting the urge to reach for her, pull her into his embrace, and kiss her full lips.

"This is harder than I ever imagined."

"I know." He referred to his own plight, not hers.

She laid her hand on his arm.

He squeezed his eyes shut, remaining very still.

"I just can't thank you enough. You've been my rock this past week." She slipped her arm around his back.

Pulling his hand from his pocket, he wrapped his arm around her. Her small frame made him feel even more protective.

She turned, wrapping both arms around his waist, and he pulled her into a full embrace. She laid her head against his chest, and he felt her relax against him.

They stood there for several minutes in the stillness of the night, just holding each other. He closed his eyes, resting his chin against the top of her head, and he prayed for her, asking for healing for her broken heart, for renewed joy, and a new hope.

Then he heard the sob and felt her whole body quiver. He quietly held her and kept praying.

≈

Tori greeted Jake with a hug as he came through her parents' front door the following morning. "Day seven of the wedding that won't end," she joked.

"Brunch and gifts." He smiled.

"Can we talk for a second?"

He nodded. "I wanted to talk to you, too, so yes."

She led him into her dad's office and closed the door. Leaning against his desk, she faced Jake. "Thanks for last night. I was a mess, and you were the best."

His face lit up at the compliment, but he shrugged it off.

"No, really. I feel like you were God's gift just to me. You knew just what to say and do to help me through one of the most painful nights of my life." She paced over to the window, seeing Marti and Kristi heading toward the front door.

"Really, it was no big deal." He joined her at the window.

"It was to me." She stood on tiptoe, placing a kiss on his cheek. "I felt like I had a big brother watching out for me." She smiled up at him. "I always wanted a brother." She bumped his shoulder in a playful manner.

He bumped her back. "Big brother, huh?"

"And we are now related in a roundabout way. So what did you want to talk to me about?"

"Two things, actually. I'd like to keep in touch with you, since we're practically related. Would you mind an occasional text or e-mail?"

"Electronic pen pals?"

"Yep."

She giggled. "Can we have an occasional phone call? Sometimes it's nice to hear a person's voice."

He nodded and smiled. "Deal." He held out his hand, and they shook on it. His warmth and kindness wasn't lost on her, nor was his smile.

"Guess we should go join the party. If she opens the cappuccino machine I registered for, I may cry." She only half joked.

"Wait, one more thing. How about a quick dinner at Mi Nidito tonight?" He grinned and gave her an irresistible puppy-dog expression. "It's my last chance until I come home for Christmas."

"I thought the guys were all going out tonight after the happy couple leaves on my—I mean their—honeymoon." She let the sarcasm flow.

"They are, but I'd much rather have Mi Nidito with you, if you're free."

She nodded. "I'm free, so you have yourself a date." Her stomach growled. "Let's go eat. As you know by now, my mom is a great cook, and brunch will not disappoint."

☙

Jake went home to his parents' after the gifts had all been opened. As he showered and got ready for his last evening with Tori, he wondered how he'd keep her in his life and revamp the way she viewed him. Big brother was never a great nickname for a guy who wanted a girl to fall for him. God had a pretty big agenda because Tori was far from recognizing him as a man she could love. He'd been praying all afternoon for answers. Seeing her a couple of times a year for a week didn't hold much promise.

He locked the front door and waited by the curb, knowing Tori was always punctual. Sure enough, not a minute or two later, her little Bug rounded the corner and putted its way toward him.

He slid into the passenger seat, and she pulled away. "Are people still lingering at your parents' house?"

"A few." She tipped her head to one side, stretching her neck. "I'm so glad this week is over."

Compassion welled up in him. "Tom said many of the things they did this week had been part of your original plans and had been borrowed by your sister."

Tori nodded. "I think that made the week all the harder for me. It felt like my wedding, only I wasn't the bride." Her smile was bittersweet.

"Did she ask?"

"She did, and I should have said no, but I've spent my life saying yes to Roni. Some habits are hard to break."

And some people are clueless. Sounded like Roni never even considered Tori or how hard this might be for her.

"I wanted a week-long wedding event since Spense and his family all lived so far away. That way the families could really get to know each other. Roni wanted it 'cause it sounded like fun."

"Tori, you really are one selfless, amazing woman."

"I didn't feel very selfless when I cried through the whole week and found myself resenting Roni for being so unoriginal."

"She didn't have to be. You'd already done all the thinking for her. I have a boss who says the quickest way to get someone to stop doing something is to do it for them."

"Yeah, he might have a point. It's all over now, though, no going back. I figured I wasn't using the plan so she might as well. I just didn't realize how hard it would be to live it out."

"My guess is this week will bring a lot of closure for you, even though it was hard and painful. Hopefully by tomorrow life will settle into some sort of normalcy."

"It's true. I've spent the last two months working alongside Roni to make this wedding happen so quickly. Getting back to a non-wedding-focused life will be nice."

Tori parked the car, finding one open space between both their parking lots. "Looks like a long wait."

"As always. I'll run and get us on the list and then meet you out front."

❧

Tori rested her head against the steering wheel and let out a long sigh. She had prayed a million prayers to get her through this past week. And she made it. Exhausted mentally, physically, and emotionally, but she'd made it. And God had been so good to provide Jake.

She climbed from her car, grabbing her purse from behind the driver's seat. She slung it over her shoulder and headed over to find Jake. He was coming out the front door. He guided her to a cement planter, and they sat on the edge. Tori felt too tired for conversation.

"You're wiped out, aren't you?"

She nodded. "As many of your damp shirts will testify, it's been an emotional week."

He chuckled. "We shouldn't have come. I'm sorry. I didn't think about how tired you might be."

"No, it's fine. Brunch is finally wearing off, and I'm starting to feel hungry."

"We'll make it an early night. And I have good news for you. I don't need a ride to the airport in the morning."

"How come?" She yawned, secretly grateful for the extra hour of sleep that would afford her.

"Apparently Colin works out that direction, so he'll drop me on his way, but thanks for your willingness."

He invited her to rest her head on him, and she took him up on his offer. They sat in silence until his name was called. "That's us." He took her hand and pulled her up with him.

Once they settled into their booth, she said, "Comfortable."

He raised an eyebrow as he dipped a tortilla chip into some salsa. "What?"

She glanced over the top of her menu. "Comfortable, another one of your attributes."

He rolled his eyes. Maybe to a guy being comfortable wasn't a compliment.

Other than the exhaustion, she felt a boatload of relief. It was over. Her dream wedding in the form of her sister's was finally over. Maybe now the peace would come.

❧

Jake hugged Tori good-bye across the gearshift knob. This wasn't the tender farewell he'd have liked, but it would have to do.

"You want to hang out when I'm here at Christmas?" How pathetic did that sound?

She looked surprised. "Sure."

"Well, until then. Here's looking at you, kid." He winked.

She laughed, and he climbed out of the yellow Bug.

"See ya, Jake." She shifted into gear and drove off. He felt certain his heart went with her, leaving a fairly large and empty hole in his chest.

five

Time might heal wounds after all. Though Tori had not believed that a few short months ago. Six weeks had passed since the wedding, and her heart had actually begun to mend. And this beautiful ninety-degree Saturday in the middle of May held some sort of hope that she'd not felt in some time.

Locking her apartment door, she headed out to her happy yellow Bug. She raised her face to the sky. "Thank You, God. I almost feel normal. Normal pre–New Year's Day and the breakup."

Her phone rang. Jake's face popped up. A silly photo of him she'd taken at Mi Nidito. She smiled and flipped her phone open. "Hey."

"Hey, you. Whatcha doing?"

"I'm meeting Roni for lunch."

"My favorite spot?" He sounded hopeful.

"No. Sorry. Chantilly Tea Room." She buckled her seat belt and started her car.

"A girly joint, huh?"

"Definitely. We usually take Mom every Mother's Day, but she and Dad are on that cruise, so we decided to take ourselves." She pulled out into traffic.

"Don't forget to raise your pinky high."

She laughed. "I won't. Anything new with you?"

"It's still cold here. Hard to believe you people are already working on your tans. The resort is closed. We're between our winter and summer seasons, so lots of renovation and cleaning going on. I won't keep you. Tell Roni to have that cousin of mine call. I've left him a couple of messages."

"I will. Have a great day, Jake." She closed her cell and held it against her cheek for a moment. They'd become great buddies during the last few weeks, and spending time on the phone with him highlighted each week. Beyond easy to talk to, he was a great listener and an encourager rolled into one solid friend.

She parked under a palo verde tree, hoping the shade would keep her car a few degrees cooler. Roni was perusing the gifts while waiting. They hugged, and the hostess led them to a lace-draped table for two.

"School's almost out." Roni arranged the cloth napkin across her gray linen pants and picked up the menu.

"I'll finish two weeks from yesterday. The kids get out a couple of days before that." She sipped the clear, cool water. The floating lemon slice gave it a hint of citrus flavor.

"I think I'm going with the special." Roni laid her menu aside, always quick and decisive.

"I'll have the chicken salad."

The waitress returned for their order.

"Any summer plans? My office is swamped. I thought you might want to make some extra money doing filing, phone work, and light secretarial stuff." Roni stirred an artificial sweetener into the apricot tea that was just placed in front of her.

"I'm not sure yet, but I'll keep your offer in mind." Why couldn't she ever just say no to her sister? Working in her office sounded as unappealing as a root canal. "Have you talked to Mom or Dad at all since they left?"

Roni smiled a sly smile. "Actually, Tom and I spoke to them this morning." Her sister acted coy.

"Is everything all right?"

"More than, Aunt Tori." Roni's smile covered a large portion of her face.

"Aunt Tori?" A stab of jealousy hit her full force. "Are you saying. . .?"

Roni nodded, and a little ladylike squeal left her lips. "We're pregnant! I'm going to be a mom!"

Be happy. But the emotions churning within were anything but. "Wow. Congratulations." She pasted a big smile on her face.

"A honeymoon baby. Can you believe it?"

"No. No I really can't. Wow." Tori kept smiling, but so much for time healing. This news hit her like a Mack truck, and her heartache was back in full force. She and Spense had planned to wait only three months before starting their family. So instead of Tori having a baby next year, it would be Roni. It was always Roni.

Her sister chatted through lunch about nurseries, names, and newborns. She wondered if she'd be able to have it all—her job and children.

"Of course you can. After all, you're Roni Wade-Nelson, woman extraordinaire. You do all things well." Tori hoped her smile hid the envy.

Pregnant. Who would have guessed it would happen so soon?

"Mom and Dad are of course thrilled. Their first grandchild."

She nodded. *Lord, help me to feel thrilled as well.* But nothing changed. Feelings of envy and self-pity swarmed around like bees.

❧

The call Jake expected rang through. Tom had called him a bit ago with the big news. Instinctively Jake knew the baby announcement would hit Tori hard. Being a wife and mom was at the top of her list—her heart's desire.

"Hi, Tori."

"They're pregnant." A sob slipped out along with the announcement. "Why can't I just be happy for them? I am a horrible person. What is wrong with me?"

His heart ached for her. "Don't beat yourself up. I know this sounds trite, but ask God to give you that happiness. Ask God to fill you to overflowing with excitement for them." He walked to his office window overlooking the mountains, which still had patches of melting snow.

"How did this happen? She used to not even want kids. First she steals my wedding, and now she takes away my chance for the first grandchild. Once again, Roni wins. Tori loses."

Why is everything a competition to you? "Tori, someday none of this will matter. One day you'll meet a man, and marrying him will be the only thing that matters. And he'll be so worth the wait that you'll thank God Spense chose someone else because what God has for you will be so much better." He didn't say that with any conceit whatsoever. He knew deep in his soul that if God ordained them to be together, it was His very best plan for both of them.

"Is that how you survived your breakup?"

"Partially. I was praying. My parents were praying. Deep down I knew if she were the one, we'd have made it. I'm believing and trusting Him, Tori. Believing He has someone phenomenal down the road just for me. A someone so much better suited to me that she'll be worth every minute I wait."

She was quiet a minute. He said nothing, hoping the truth of his words would sink in.

"That is a pretty impassioned speech."

He smiled. "It came from the heart."

"I don't doubt that, but do you ever doubt that it will really happen?"

"Yeah. Then I go back to my Bible and read how much God loves me and about the abundant life He has planned for me. Abundant. Above all I can ask, think, or imagine. What can be better than that?"

"I don't know. But I want what you're waiting for."

"Then ask, Tori, and keep asking."

"Ask, seek, knock?" He heard her car door slam and her alarm beep.

"Exactly. Where are you?"

"Just getting home from my lunch with Roni. I planned to lock myself away for the weekend and cry, but you've inspired me to dig through the Word for myself and do some praying."

"A much more productive idea than wallowing." His heart lightened. He glanced upward and mouthed, *Thank You*. Some of his prayers for her were already taking effect.

"Sometimes wallowing just feels good."

"You're right. And sometimes it's time to give it up and move forward, eyes on the Lord."

" 'Onward, Christian Soldiers'? Did you sing that as a kid?"

"Yes, in Vacation Bible School. Hey, are you sitting down?"

"I am now. On the couch. Feet up on the coffee table."

He pictured the scene. "I have a proposition for you." Jake had chewed on this idea for a few weeks, and now was the time to present it to Tori.

"A proposition? Sounds mysterious."

"Simple actually. Come to Idaho for the summer."

"I can't afford it."

"My accounts-payable clerk has maternity leave starting

the second week of June. She returns the first week of August. Come up here and work. I can get you a free room at the resort." He shot up another prayer. After continued silence, he asked, "Tori, did I lose you?" He glanced at his cell to see if they were still connected. "Can you hear me? Say something."

"I'm here. I just don't know what to say."

"Last time we talked, you said you still had no summer plans."

"That's true." She sounded hesitant.

"Think of it as a reprieve from life. You come up here, get out of the heat, and away from constant reminders of endless hurts." *Give me a chance with you.*

ஐ

The idea was growing on her. "Keep going."

"A retreat, if you will. We'll do some exploring, and you can come fall in love."

Her heart sped up. "Fall in love?" Surely he didn't mean with him. He was great as a brother, held huge possibilities as a best friend, but. . .

"With Idaho." He laughed, drawing her laughter.

"So I'd have a job and a place to live?"

"Two months to escape the hurt and heal."

It felt like he tossed her a lifeline. "I've never done accounts payable."

"You can come up as soon as you're out of school, and I'll have Allison train you. She'll have about a week to get you trained and set up for the summer. You're a math teacher. How hard can it be?"

She giggled. "You might be surprised. What if I let you down?"

"Then I call a temp agency—quick." His attitude calmed

her fears. "I need a temporary payable clerk. You need a summer job and are a math whiz, I might add. That to me equals a perfect equation."

"That to me might equal disaster. And I never said or even implied that I'm a math whiz. You met me and know by now how very average I am."

"That's what most of us are, Tori. Average, ordinary, normal. No shame in that." He paused. "Come on. What's the worst that can happen?"

"I just don't want to let you down." For some reason, what Jake thought of her mattered.

"The only way you'll let me down is if you say no."

She smiled. "Thank you, Jake. You're one in a million."

"Only one in a million, not a billion?"

"I'll have to think about that one."

"So. . . ?" He drew the word out. "What about the job?"

"Honestly, it sounds perfect. Some time to get away, clear my head. Leave the jealousy and comparisons far behind." She paced across the small apartment living room. "But I was thinking of doing some house hunting this summer."

He swallowed loud enough for it to carry over the phone line. "House hunting?"

"It's a buyer's market. Good time to take the plunge. I didn't before because I didn't think I'd be here that long."

"Maybe you won't. Who knows what God has in store?"

She thought his response odd. Who *ever* knows what God has in store?

"Put the house hunting on hold. Spend a summer in paradise, and I don't mean Hawaii."

She giggled. "I've not seen this persistent side of you before. Are you always this pushy?" She loved the freedom they had with each other to say whatever was on their minds.

"I'm sorry. No, I'm not normally dubbed as pushy. I just know all the talk of babies and the upcoming wedding date will be hard."

She hadn't even considered how miserable July would be as the date drew closer. She sucked in a deep breath. "You know what, you're right. It will be a miserable summer if I stay in Tucson. It may be a miserable summer anyway. Are you prepared for more soggy shirts?"

He laughed. "Ready, willing, and able."

"Then Jake Matthews, I accept your offer of employment."

"That's great. You won't regret it. When can you start?"

"I check out for the summer two weeks from yesterday. I'll load my car Saturday and leave Sunday. How long will it take me to get there?"

"Two long days of driving. Why don't you fly? It's not safe for you to be on the road alone for that distance."

"Now you sound like my dad. You are turning into too many relatives rolled into one." She giggled. "For a two-month stay, I'll need more than a couple of suitcases can hold, so flying is out. I have a cell phone and an emergency roadside service. What more can a girl need?"

"A travel companion," was his dry reply. "Hey, you didn't even ask about the salary."

"Doesn't matter. You've convinced me this is an answer to avoid a tough and painful summer. I've got to go. Lots to do in the next couple of weeks."

He chuckled. "Once you make a decision, you're off and running."

"Don't know if it's good or bad, but that's me. Talk to you soon?"

"*See* you soon." She heard the excitement in his voice, and she was excited to see him again, too.

six

Tom, Roni, Dad, and Mom all showed up on her doorstep early Saturday morning. She had packed up her whole apartment since the lease was up June first. She'd originally planned to stay an extra month and marry Spense in July. Now she'd move her stuff to storage, and when she returned from Idaho, she'd stay with her parents until she found a place to buy.

"I can't believe you're leaving for the summer." Roni stuck out her bottom lip. "How come you'll work for Jake, but not for me?"

"Accounting is more up my alley than a file clerk." She picked up a box and headed out the door to the U-Haul truck her dad had rented for the day.

Roni followed, also carrying a box. "I don't know if I should be lifting. Anyway, I was hoping you'd help me decorate the nursery." She handed her box up to their dad.

"Sorry. Won't be around, but I'm sure Mom would love to help you." More certain than ever she'd made the right decision, Tori headed back into the house for another box.

"Mom, do you think it's okay if I lift?" Pregnancy had turned her twin into a whiny, pampered princess.

"I don't know, honey...."

Tori carried another box out, and when she returned, they still continued to debate the pros and cons of Roni lifting.

She faced her sister. "Forget it. I don't need your help. Go sit down somewhere and stop whining!" She grabbed another box, noting the shocked expression both her sister and her mother wore before heading back out the door.

Tom rounded up his old roommates to help move the furniture, and Roni left shortly after Tori's outburst. At the end of the day, all Tori wanted was a hot bath and an early bedtime. That, however, would have to follow a family farewell dinner, which she'd love to ditch.

On the drive from the storage unit to her parents', she allowed herself to call Jen. "These international calls are expensive, so I can only afford a five-minute call, but I had to update you." She shared her sisterly meltdown.

"Is this the first time you've noticed that she's a pampered prima donna? I've been telling you that forever."

"I know, but she's my sister. Hard to hear the worst, but I'm seeing it more and more. She's a spoiled brat, and I enable her. Anyway, enough complaining. Tomorrow I head north, and my mom is sending me off in style with a fancy breakfast. I can't believe I'm not going to see you until the very end of the summer. Over a year! We've never gone that long."

"I miss you so much, but this has been the experience of a lifetime! I will see you at the end of summer. I think we've used your five minutes, so we'd better hang up, but you can call me every day while in Idaho."

"I will. I promise. Bye, Jen." She clicked her phone shut.

Tori arrived at her parents' with time to shower before dinner. When she came out, the five of them gathered around the table.

"Honey, is everything all right?" her mother asked as she handed Tori the mashed potatoes. She'd cooked Tori's favorite meal of roast beef.

Tori took the potatoes and spooned some onto her plate.

"Yes, why?" Though she knew what prompted the question.

"You were awfully short with Roni earlier. That's so unlike you."

How honest could she be with them? The bottom line was that Tori was angry at Roni for taking her year, borrowing her wedding ideas, and now having the first grandchild. And her parents were so busy being happy for Roni, they never took her into consideration. Didn't anyone care that this was the worst year of her life?

"The past two weeks have been crazy busy. I'm moving from living an hour away from Mexico to living an hour away from Canada, albeit for only two months. Everything in my life has changed since January first—my relational status, where I live, my life goals."

"You hurt my feelings." Roni always let her know right where she stood.

"Maybe we've hurt Tori's feelings, too," her dad spoke up. "It's been a hard year for her, and we've all gotten so caught up in Roni's whirlwind life that nobody bothered to check on you very often. When I did, you always said that you were fine. Please forgive us if we forgot your pain for even a single second. We will all miss you so much." Her dad rose and came to her chair, pulling her up into his bear hug.

The evening ended with tears, hugs, and certainly some healing. She and Roni both apologized to each other, and Tori felt better about leaving in the morning now that some family issues were resolved.

૨⚬

Jake called Tori every couple of hours on her drive up. She accused him of being worse than an old momma hen but didn't seem to mind. They chatted about scenery she passed and how unique each state was. God, the Creator, did an amazing job, and they were both in awe of Him.

Feeling like a kid waiting for his birthday, he anticipated her arrival. As the time drew near, he watched out his office window for her car to top the hill. He'd have to fight off the urge to run to her, whisk her into his arms, and soundly kiss her. Instead, he'd strive for casual, nonchalant. Like she'd believe that after his 457 phone calls.

His cell rang. Tori's pretty face graced his screen. "Everything okay?"

"I'm not sure. I feel like I'm on the wrong road. Did I miss it somehow?"

He laughed, tugging at his tie. He shut his office blinds and traded his work attire for casual as they talked. "We're at the top, the end of the line, so you didn't miss us. But nine and a half miles feels long on that windy twenty-five-mile-per-hour road."

"You aren't kidding. I feel like I've been twisting and turning forever. I did see a deer, which almost makes this road worth it. I think I'm here!"

"I'll be right out." He'd spotted her yellow Bug just as she shouted her arrival. He made a beeline for her car.

"Where do I park?"

He pointed to the underground parking and followed her down there. When she exited the car, he was right there to greet her. She wrapped her arms around his neck and his arms circled her waist. He tucked his nose into her neck. She smelled as good as she looked—some flowery, feminine scent. Finally, he forced himself to loosen his hold.

"It's so good to be here. I'm sick of that car." She glanced around the empty garage, backing out of his hold. "Where is everyone? This doesn't look good for business."

"We're actually between seasons. Our summer season

won't officially start for a couple more weeks. Come on"—he motioned with his head—"I want you to see the place before daylight disappears completely." He pulled her against his side for another quick hug. He couldn't help himself. "I'm so glad you made it safe and sound."

"Me, too. Ohh, it's beautiful," she said as they exited the garage. She spun around, trying to take it all in. "Now those are some mountains." She faced west, noting the peaks rising about the lodge. "It's adorable. Looks like a little Swiss mountain village." She pulled her sweater more tightly around her.

"You cold?"

Her nod was the perfect excuse to wrap his arm around her shoulders. She shivered against him. "Where's your coat?"

"Packed somewhere in my car. The temp was ninety-five degrees when I left Tucson. What is it here?" Her nose had grown red.

"You Arizona people are wimps. I'm sure it's in the mid-forties." He was comfortable in his jeans and sweatshirt.

"That's a temperature we usually only experience in the middle of the night. At that point, I'm sound asleep and don't have a clue." She shook her head, her blond hair swinging this way and that. "What have I gotten myself into?" She laughed.

&

They passed through the little village, and he told her about each shop. The place felt magical somehow as she imagined the boardwalk laden with vacationers and the little shops bursting with business. The cold air rejuvenated her. She felt alive. Coming here was a good decision. She felt it deep inside.

Jake led her over by the lifts, and they looked out over the valley. Twilight neared. She shivered and her teeth chattered. He stood behind her, wrapping his arms around her, pulling her back against him.

"We should get you inside." Warm breath danced against her cheek.

"Not yet. I'm savoring the sights and sounds." *And sensations.* Her heart beat a little faster at his nearness. This was something new, something she wasn't sure how to deal with. He rested his chin on the top of her head. She felt the steady rhythm of his heart beating and the unsteadiness of her own.

He raised his arm over her shoulder and pointed out Lake Pend Oreille. "It's spelled much different than it's pronounced. It's French, and you say it 'Pon-duh-ray.'"

She relaxed. The weird chemistry thing a few moments ago had to be her imagination. He acted normal as could be. She focused on what he was saying.

"The lake is the largest natural body of fresh water in Idaho and one of the largest in the western United States. It is more than forty-three miles in length, six and a half miles in width at its widest point, and has more than one hundred and eleven miles of shoreline. Most amazingly, the lake is more than eleven hundred feet deep in places and is the home to a variety of fish, including world-record-size Kamloops and mackinaw."

"You lost me when fish came into the conversation."

He laughed, still holding her close. "Sorry."

"So, Sandpoint is located in the panhandle of northern Idaho?"

"Yep, sandwiched between Montana to the east and Washington to the west. We're on the northern shore of Lake Pend Oreille and at the foot of the Selkirk Mountains.

This resort sits in the middle of the Selkirks."

"It's beautiful," she said with quiet awe.

"I told you so. I knew you'd fall in love."

"That you did." *But you didn't warn me it might be with you.* His breath sent goose bumps over her flesh. She shivered. He tightened his hold as if to ward off her chill. Little did he know, he was the cause of it. She wiggled out of his arms, though she might like resting in them for who knew how long. Maybe forever? "I'd better go unload my car before it's completely dark outside."

She strode toward the garage. Jake followed. What in the world was happening to her? He seemed oblivious to any change in her, but her senses were heightened to him.

"I remember my first view of Sandpoint as I drove over the Long Bridge that crosses the lake," he recalled as they trudged back to the garage.

She smiled at him. His passion for Idaho lit up his face.

"From that vantage point, I got a sense of the size of the lake, the beauty of the surrounding mountains, and the idyllic setting of the town. That view sold me on Sandpoint forever."

"Sounds like you're talking about a woman, not a place." As they approached her car, she clicked the unlock button. "I admit I was wrong. There is definitely a lot more than potatoes here."

Jake grabbed the largest suitcase after handing her a smaller one. She pulled out the handle, threw a tote bag over her shoulder, and followed Jake into the elevator, which dumped them out at the lodge's lobby and registration area. While Jake got the keys, Tori's gaze lingered over the large expanse. It was beautiful with a large stone fireplace on one side and overstuffed leather chairs arranged around it. The staircase caught her eye with a highly polished, knotty pine railing.

Once Jake stowed her luggage inside the apartment, he left her to unpack. She pulled her cell phone from her purse and pushed number five. "Jen, you would not believe this place!"

"Well hello to you, too! So you're glad you went?"

"I think so." She hesitated.

"Wait. You were just bubbling over with excitement. Now you only think so?"

Did she want to confess that she might have more than friendship-type feelings for Jake? Naw. "This is a high-class place." She'd thrown one of the suitcases across the bed and started unloading her clothes into the empty drawers in the dresser. "Everything is lovely. My apartment is adorable. Small living room, kitchenette, nice size bed and bath all furnished with a cabin kind of look. You know, lots of rich wood and a homey feel. And boy did God smile on this area. His handprints are all over the beauty here. It's just awesome."

"I'm glad for you. I hope you have an extra wonderful summer. I'm praying for that. Now why the hesitation?"

"Jake. Comfortable Jake. Hugging him was comfortable. His arms wrapped around me—completely comfortable. His smile and the way we joke—comfortable. The way he looked at me—"

"Comfortable," Jen finished for her.

"He felt like an old sweater I might pull out on a cold winter day. A dear friend. Someone who warms you inside. I mean, other than you, he's my best friend."

"All that sounds good, not bad." Jen wasn't tracking with her.

"Today all that was different. Not for him so much, I don't

think, but for me. Some button in me switched on, and I've started thinking of him like a man."

"Ohhh. . ." She dragged out the word in a the-light-bulb-has-turned-on kind of way. "He is definitely a man. I've never doubted it for a minute—not for a minute, girlfriend. And I think that's great. You're slowly getting over Spense and waking up to other possibilities."

I don't think it's great at all. I never want to hurt like that again. Not ever.

❧

"Hey, how's your first week been?" Jake popped in to see her on Friday afternoon. "Has Allison got you trained and ready to take the reins?"

Allison nodded. "She's good to go. Met the whole crew. Has done every task at least once. Took good notes. Caught on quickly. My baby can come anytime now because Tori knows the ropes and this place will survive without me."

"Sounds good, but surviving without you may be tough. Hey, do you mind if I steal Tori away a couple of hours early?"

Allison shook her head, a surprised expression etched across her features.

"We're old friends." He set her straight. "Thought I'd take her into Sandpoint for the rest of the afternoon, if you don't mind."

Allison shook her head. "Not at all." She focused brown eyes on Tori. "You go. I'll finish up here."

"You sure?" Tori crinkled her forehead in that cute way she did.

Allison nodded. "Go."

Tori rose and followed him out of the office.

"Is it my imagination, or are you avoiding me?" he asked

once they were in the garage and heading toward his SUV.

"Busy week. I took notes all day and went home and studied them each evening to solidify everything."

He opened the passenger door, Tori climbed in, and then he shut it. Once he climbed in his side, he continued, "We talked more when you were fifteen hundred miles away."

She smiled—a sweet, sincere smile, and he knew he'd forgive her for anything. He pulled out of the garage, and they started their trek down the mountain.

"I always hate the first week of a new job. I wanted to give it my undivided attention."

"All right. I'll let you off the hook this time, but I assumed we'd hang out all the time since you're only here a couple of months. Don't let me down," he warned in a gruff voice. *I only have so much time to convince you I'm the guy.*

"We will. I promise. So, Jakey, no pouting or whining this afternoon." She laughed—a glee-filled sound he'd never tire of—and popped him on the thigh with the bright pink ponytail holder she'd had on her wrist.

He glanced her direction, raised his brows, and grabbed the elastic hair piece, shoving it in his pocket. Even though she appeared playful, he thought he caught a note of apprehension in her tone, but decided to let it drop. Was she sorry she came? "How does a little dinner on the waterfront sound? There is a place called Spuds with an outdoor patio."

"Sounds perfect. Outdoor dining isn't something we do much in Tucson during the summer, and as you know, water is scarce in the desert, so of course I love both."

When they got to the restaurant, Jake requested the back deck. The hostess led them across the worn wood floor to their table. Jake pulled out a green patio chair for Tori and took the menus, placing one in front of her.

"This is perfect. Water, mountains in the backdrop, and a crystal blue sky."

He smiled up from the menu at her words of approval. He was batting 50 percent. She liked the place—now for the man. . .

They sat side by side facing the water. Just beyond their table and the wooden railing was a dock full of boats. After dinner they walked along the downtown streets and popped into a few shops. He resisted the urge to hold her hand. He'd have to be extra careful. He wondered if he'd given away his feelings and that's why she was avoiding him. Maybe she knew how he really felt and that friendship was the last thing on his mind.

seven

"Jen, you have to come up for a long weekend. It's the cutest place on earth. Sandpoint has all these wonderful little boutiques. I'm not even a shopper and can't wait to go back." Tori propped her feet on her coffee table and leaned back against the sofa cushions.

"Are you chatting incessantly to avoid any question I might ask about a certain man that is all man?"

"Possibly."

"Not gonna work. Talk to me, girlfriend."

"He's charming, and you're right—very attractive. I'm not sure how I missed it in the beginning. He's filled with lots of wonderful characteristics that Spense lacked. I think he's exactly the kind of guy I could fall for." Tori walked over to her window. She'd fallen in love with the view—the man could be next.

"Then fall, girlfriend, fall. I don't think Jake's the kind of guy who'd even look at another woman."

"I don't think so either, but I wouldn't have guessed it with Spense, so who really knows?"

"I would have."

"But you never liked him."

"And for good reason. Now back to Jake. What's keeping you from taking the plunge?"

"Fear, distance. A signed contract to teach starting in August in Arizona. Nothing about this would work. His life is here. Mine is there."

"You were moving to start a marriage with Spense. Why not Jake?"

"To the Twin Cities. That's different. I'm not a small-town girl. Two months—yes. Twelve, year after year, I'm not so sure."

"For a great guy, I'd move almost anywhere." Jen had a wistful note in her voice. "Think about it, Tori. Maybe this is the happily ever after you've been dreaming of."

"And maybe it's a summer romance that will end with a change in the weather. What are we even talking about? It's one-sided at best."

Though Rachel in the payroll office kept mentioning the way Jake looked at Tori when he thought no one was looking. *He's got it for you, girl.* Rachel repeated that phrase almost daily. And every time she did, Tori's heart sped up, though she always replied with a "no way."

"Maybe so, but you'll never know how one-sided if you don't give him a chance."

"What do you want me to do?"

"Stop running and let him catch you."

"Okay. I will, but only because you're dead wrong." But a part of her hoped she was the one who was wrong.

After hanging up with Jen, Tori wandered downstairs, half hoping to run into Jake. She brought a magazine down and settled into one of the beige leather chairs at the base of the stairs near the fireplace. After reading for a while, she headed into the Mojo Coyote Café for an afternoon hit of caffeine. Still no sign of Jake.

What would the old Tori do—before this ridiculous crush? She'd call him or march into his office and throw out an idea for some fun. Exiting the café on her way to do just that, she spotted him, big as life, hugging another woman!

Tori froze just inside the lobby, her gaze locked on the affectionate couple. *Don't stare, Tori, it's rude.* Her mother's well-modulated tone chimed in her head. Polite or not, she couldn't stop gawking.

Jake hugged the leggy brunette, kissed her cheek, and said something near her ear. They both laughed. An ugly something rose up in Tori, and she felt torn between ripping the woman's eyes out and stomping off in a rage. She, of course, did neither.

"Tori, come meet an old friend of mine." She forced her feet to carry her toward them.

"Old?" The woman reprimanded him with her eyes, her beautiful bright blue eyes fringed with long black lashes.

"Tori, Liddy. Liddy, Tori."

Liddy turned a warm, perfect smile on her. She hoped hers was as gracious. Something about this woman made her feel mousy and plain. Invisible. Just like she felt around Roni at times.

His arm remained around Liddy's waist. He obviously saw nothing wrong with his behavior. *And why should he? I mean, we're friends. Friends. Nothing more, except in my overactive imagination.* Disappointment fell on her like a summer rain.

A very tall and quite handsome fellow stopped next to Tori, closing the circle.

"Tori, meet Gordy. Gordy, Tori."

His large hand engulfed hers. "Nice to meet you." His smile, several-hundred watts bright, was focused on Liddy.

Of course.

"Hey, babe, did you proposition him yet?" He winked at Jake.

Relief washed over Tori as the woman moved from Jake's side to Gordy's. *I like him more than I thought.*

Jake wasn't sure, but he'd have bet he saw jealousy in Tori's eyes. The thought made him smile. Good sign.

"So what do you say?" Gordy asked Jake.

"About the proposition?" His brows furrowed together.

"Nice meeting you both. Now, if you'll excuse me." Tori turned to walk away.

Jake grabbed her arm. "Wait, this might involve you."

"Me?" A wary expression blanketed her face. "I, uh, don't do propositions," she stammered. "Sorry."

"This one might interest you," Gordy spoke up. "Ever been in a float plane?"

Tori shook her head.

"It's glorious!" Liddy beamed a big smile on Tori. "Like floating on clouds. We're trying to get Jake to fly us to Coeur d'Alene. You have to come as well." Long french-manicured fingers patted Tori's arm. "You must join us."

Tori glanced his way. "You fly?"

He nodded.

"Wow." She was impressed, and that was enough for him.

"Sure." He shrugged. "Why not? Tomorrow after church?"

Everyone nodded their agreement.

"We're headed down the mountain for dinner." Gordy slapped Jake's back. "Meet you at the lake after church tomorrow." Gordy and Liddy walked away holding hands. A longing hit him square in the heart. One he never expected to feel again.

He glanced at Tori. She, too, watched the couple retreat. "How do you know them?"

Jake smiled. "I was the best man at their wedding. Gordy and I have been buds since third grade, roomed together in college. We go way back."

"His wife is beautiful, so tall and statuesque." Tori studied his face.

"Yeah, I guess. Not really my type. She's more like a sister to me, so I never paid much attention." He scratched his chin. "They were one of the lucky ones. Met their freshman year of college, fell in love their sophomore year, and married their junior year. None of the messy dating scene for them."

"And all the heartbreak it entails. I was almost one of those, marrying my first and only love. . . ." Her voice sounded wistful. "Don't know if I'll ever be ready for that roller-coaster ride again."

"You will. You know time and all that yada yada." Jake shoved his hands into the pockets of his khaki shorts. He didn't stand a chance if she still grieved over Spense.

"Says the man who hasn't gotten back in the saddle for five years." She raised a brow in challenge.

"Touché. You got me there." *But what you don't know is I'm finally ready. Lord, please don't let it take her five years.* "So do you want to ride to church with me in the morning?"

"That would be great since I have no idea where I'm going." Her smile never failed to get a response from somewhere in the area of his gut.

"Meet me here at nine. The dress is casual."

She nodded.

On impulse he kissed her cheek, keeping his fisted hands restrained in his pockets. "I'm really glad you came."

"Me, too."

Something in her eyes—some sort of tenderness—caught the breath in his throat. His heart beat harder. Did she have any idea what she did to him? His eyes betrayed him and wandered to her lips—ripe, inviting, kissable.

He had to break the tension, or he'd end up kissing her

for sure. "I've got to run. I'll probably burn some midnight oil tonight so I can have tomorrow off. I'm glad you're going with us to Coeur d'Alene."

"Me, too." She paused and looked down. "Are you sure you want me intruding on your time with old friends? I'd understand—"

"No way. You're not getting out of this now."

She raised her gaze to meet his. "But—"

He laid his fingers across her lips to quiet her protests— the gesture more intimate than he'd intended. Their gazes locked, her expression wide-eyed and vulnerable. He let his hand drop from her mouth slowly. She raised her head a bit, and her slightly parted lips drew him like a bee to a flower.

His slid his hand under her hair behind her neck and applied the slightest pressure. She leaned into him willingly. Their lips met in a symphony of perfectly blended notes. After the kiss, he placed a hand on each side of her face. Her expression held the same wonderment that he felt.

"You okay with this change of status?"

She nodded. "I'm scared."

"Me, too—at least a little bit, but I won't ever do to you what Spense did."

"I know." He heard the doubt that lingered between them.

"The only way I can prove myself is time. Are you in for the long haul?"

Again she hesitated. "I think so."

He wished she was more certain, but he was certain enough for the both of them. Unable to resist, he kissed her again, this time a quick peck. "You run along, or I'll never get my desk cleared for tomorrow."

She laid her hand over his and turned her face into his palm, planting a kiss there. Then she smiled up at him. "I could stay and help."

He shook his head. "You'd be more of a distraction. But tomorrow I'm all yours for the whole day."

He watched her disappear up the staircase. Not how he expected the day to turn out, but he had no complaints. None at all. "Thanks, God," he whispered on the way to his office.

ঽ

"Hey, Tor," Jen answered her cell phone on the second ring.

"He kissed me! I mean he *kissed* me." The giddiness Tori felt floated across the miles.

"Wow! Sounds like you hated every second of it," Jen joked.

"All I can say is, 'Spense who?'" Tori paced around her little apartment, way too much excitement churning her insides for her to land somewhere.

Jen laughed.

"It's been a long time since life felt this magical. Thanks for encouraging me to come."

"What are friends for, if not to nag?"

They talked another few minutes and said good night.

Tori floated through her bedtime routine, reliving the kiss again and again. A kiss more exciting and passionate than she'd experienced before. She gazed at herself in the mirror, her color high, her eyes bright. She'd only ever kissed one man—until tonight. She touched her lips and smiled. Suddenly none of the obstacles like distance and small towns mattered.

She slept like a rock and awoke with anticipation flowing through her veins. A day with Jake. What could be more perfect? She spent extra time deciding what to wear, applying makeup, and fixing her hair. She wanted to look her very best for Jake. Jake—suddenly his name danced through her heart like a well-loved song. Jake and Tori. She liked the sound of them linked together as a couple. Were they a couple?

He waited at the bottom of the stairs for her. As she walked down, their gazes locked. His expression reflected his joy just at seeing her. The closer she came to him, the harder her heart pounded. He held out his hand, and she placed hers in his open palm. When she took the last step to the floor, he pulled her into his arms. "Good morning."

"Good morning." The two simple words sounded breathless.

He leaned in for another kiss, and she eagerly tipped her face toward his. The kiss was long and deep. When it ended, his eyes resembled a pool of melted chocolate.

"I had to make sure."

"Make sure?" The unsteadiness of her voice bore witness to the power of his kiss.

"That last night wasn't a fluke. That I hadn't imagined the power and wonder of your kiss."

Her cheeks grew warm. She lowered her gaze to his Adam's apple.

"Don't be embarrassed. We have a real connection—a God-given attraction. And don't worry, there will be no more first-thing-in-the-morning, knock-your-socks-off kind of kisses. I'd never get anything done." He kissed her nose, dropped his arms from around her, and took her hand, leading her to his SUV parked just out the front door of the lodge.

As Tori settled into his passenger seat, she decided that starting each day with a kiss like that would be bliss for a married couple. Dare she dream that far ahead?

❧

After the church service ended and they were back in his

SUV, Jake shared his heart. "Tori, I need to apologize to you. I shouldn't have kissed you with such abandonment, and the Lord really dealt with me this morning."

"What do you mean?" Those frown lines appeared between her brows. The ones he found so adorable.

"God doesn't want us focusing on our physical attraction. We need to put the emphasis on growing our friendship."

She nodded. "So no more kissing?"

Was that disappointment he heard? He smiled and reached for her hand. "For now. If we kept heading in that direction, how long before we'd cross lines God didn't intend us to cross?"

"You're right, of course. I've always been the one to set and enforce physical limits. This is new territory for me." She didn't look his direction, but focused on her hands in her lap.

He lifted her chin with his index finger until their eyes met. "Tori, this isn't rejection. It's conviction. Believe me, there is nothing I'd rather do than kiss you four or five hundred times a day, but I want this relationship to honor God from the get-go. Don't you?"

"Of course. And. . ." She paused and seemed to weigh her words with care.

"And?"

"I'd love to kiss you several hundred times a day, too." She said the words quickly. Pink highlighted her cheeks.

"They were quite enjoyable." He grinned, and the pink hue tinting her cheeks darkened. "Best I've had."

"Really?"

He nodded, realizing how fragile she was emotionally. Spense had broken more than her heart. He'd shattered her self-confidence as well.

"I'll be saving all my kisses for you," Jake promised. "You

do the same, and one day when the time is right, I'll kiss you a thousand times a day if I've a mind to." He winked. "Because there's nothing I'd rather do." He squeezed her hand. "Nothing."

Relief washed over her features.

He did kiss the tip of her nose, then turned in his seat to face forward and started his car. "So you'll forgive me for starting us off on the wrong foot?" He backed out of his parking space and followed the line of cars through the parking lot.

"Do you think kissing is wrong before marriage?" Her head tilted to one side.

"No. It was the way I kissed you that was wrong. It was too raw and passionate. Too physical. It stirred up too many other desires. And because I have that tendency with you, I'm taking a giant step backward. Everything about you attracts me, and I can't give in to my flesh. I've got to keep this pure and honoring to God because I want His blessing on us."

"Jake, when did you know that you liked me?"

He glanced her direction as he pulled onto the street. "From the beginning I've always known"—he spoke softly— "that you were the one."

eight

Jake pulled into a parking lot next to the lake. "There she is." He pointed to an orange and yellow plane floating on the water.

"It's small." Tori tried to sound nonchalant, but inside she felt fearful. And she hated that about herself—always cautious, always afraid. She sucked in a deep breath and refused to give in to the controlling emotion. *I can do all things through Christ. I can do all things through Christ.* She repeated the verse over and over.

"Six passenger." He waved, and Tori followed his gaze. Gordy and Liddy were just climbing out of some big, fancy black car.

As they walked toward them, Gordy hollered, "Thanks for doing this, man."

Jake nodded.

"You're a doll." Liddy smiled and turned her gaze to Tori. "I'm so glad you're joining us. Have you ridden in a float plane before?"

"No." Tori shook her head. Apparently Liddy hadn't been listening yesterday when Gordy asked her the same question. Somehow that didn't surprise Tori.

"You will love it. We'll fly so low that you can see and enjoy everything."

Tori's stomach twisted. "Sounds glorious," she lied, quoting Liddy's words from their prior conversation.

The men had wandered out on the dock and were

checking things out on the plane.

"Jake is a wonderful pilot. Very thorough. He has a mental checklist that he goes through before he'll take Arabella up for a flight."

Mental checklist! I'd rather he have a written one. How many times do I forget something. . .? More gut-wrenching fear settled into her midsection. Throwing up became a distinct possibility.

Liddy chatted about shopping in Coeur d'Alene, their college days, and Jake in general. Tori listened and nodded, praying through most of it for their impending flight. Finally, Jake motioned for them to join him and Gordy out on the dock. Tori followed Liddy on shaky and unsteady legs. She eyed Jake's plane as they drew closer. It had a front propeller and looked like a normal plane to her, but it was mounted on two big floats, and there were no wheels in sight.

"Checklist complete." Jake smiled at her. "You want to sit in the front with me?"

She nodded, no longer trusting her voice. *Sure, that way I can have a bird's-eye view if we go down.* Could anyone else hear her heart pounding?

Jake held her hand as she climbed up the ladder and into the plane. He leaned in and whispered, "Don't be afraid. It's fun."

Her gaze shot to his. How did he know?

"You're shaking," he whispered with a wink.

Once inside the plane, she made her way to the front passenger seat. Yep, bird's-eye view. The huge windshield across the front of the plane let her see for miles. She buckled her seat belt, pulled it as tight as possible, and leaned back, taking a few deep breaths while the others boarded.

Tori marveled at all the buttons and gauges—more than

a dozen of each. As Jake settled into his seat, she pointed at the instrument panel. "How can you possibly remember what they all do?"

"I remember. I promise." He laughed and handed her a pair of headphones. "We all get a pair." He handed two to Gordy, who sat right behind her. "They help block the engine noise and enable us to talk to one another." He slipped his into place.

Tori followed suit. They were bulky and very official looking. A microphone curved around in front of her chin. She tested them out. "Can everybody hear me?"

Three yeses echoed through her earphones.

Jake flipped a few switches, and before long the engine jumped to life. It was loud, even with the headset. The plane glided over the water, feeling much like a boat did.

"Sounds like a lawn mower," Tori spoke into the microphone. "You sure this thing can fly?"

All three of her companions belly laughed. About then they lifted off the water. Other than her death grip on her seat, she felt perfectly at ease. Yeah right.

The three of them chatted about old college friends, who they'd seen or heard from, and what people were up to. Tori appreciated the time. At first she prayed, and then she began to relax. This wasn't too bad. She leaned forward to see better. Liddy was right—nothing was quite like this. And she'd have missed it all if she'd let her fear win out. She smiled, raising her eyes toward heaven, and mouthed, *Thanks, Lord.*

By the time they landed in Coeur d'Alene, Tori had actually completely relaxed, which amazed her. The more she'd thanked and praised God in her head, the freer she felt. Once on the water, they taxied toward a restaurant Liddy wanted to try. Tori shook her head. The whims of the rich. They'd flown to a different town just to eat lunch.

☙

"What a great day," Liddy enthused as Jake set the plane back down on Lake Pend Oreille.

"It was, wasn't it?" He glanced at Tori. Hers was the only answer that concerned him.

She nodded and smiled. "It was—a wonderful day."

"I can never get enough of those little shops." Liddy stretched and yawned.

"The back seats of this plane testify to the truth of that statement." Gordy pointed to the piles of bags filling the back row of Arabella.

Liddy giggled. "A guilty pleasure."

Jake brought the plane to a halt against the side of the dock, jumped out, and grabbed a rope, securing them with a sailor's knot to a wood post.

Then he helped first Tori and then Liddy out of the plane. Gordy began to hand Jake bag after shopping bag, which he lined up along the edge of the wood-planked dock, secretly glad Tori wasn't a die-hard shopper.

"Are all these ours?" Gordy asked Liddy. "Didn't Tori buy anything?"

"I'm a teacher, so my main purchases are groceries and things for my classroom. No money left in my budget for much else," Tori admitted honestly.

Jake liked that about her.

"A woman who understands budgeting? Hang on to this one, Jake," Gordy encouraged.

Jake glanced at Tori, but she had looked away. Probably embarrassed, so he ignored Gordy's comment all together. "All done." He finished with the plane, grabbed a few of the shopping bags, handed a couple to Tori, and they all headed back toward the parking lot, each toting several shopping bags.

After stowing everything in the trunk, Liddy again thanked him for a great day. She kissed his cheek. "You are the best, dahling. Thank you ever so much." She chimed in some fake accent that Jake couldn't place.

Jake and Gordy exchanged the same handshake they'd been doing since junior high. "Yes, thanks ever so much for breaking my bank." He imitated the way Liddy had just spoken.

Liddy and Gordy both hugged Tori before driving off. He and Tori stood waving good-bye until they pulled out of the parking lot.

"Did you really have fun?" Jake inspected her closely, wanting the truth, not a polite response.

"I did."

He must have looked skeptical when he narrowed his eyes.

"I promise." She made the little scout's honor sign with her fingers.

Jake grabbed her hand, and they crossed the paved expanse to his SUV. "You don't care for fancy restaurants, and you don't shop. How could you have enjoyed yourself?" He opened the passenger door.

She wrapped her arms around his neck, a playful gleam in her eye. "I was with you." She planted a loud, wet kiss on his cheek. "And I'm pretty sure anywhere with you means an enjoyable time for me." She kissed his other cheek and climbed into the car.

His mind urged him to plant another kiss on her lips, just one more deep, slow kiss, but he had to obey. He stepped back and closed her door. When God asked him for something, it's either now or never. He'd choose now.

Jake climbed into the driver's side and started his car. He reached over and took her hand. "I feel the same way. Wherever you are is where I want to be." He raised her hand to his lips and kissed it. "Wherever." He backed out of the parking lot, and they headed toward Schweitzer Mountain.

The ride up the mountain was in contented silence. He'd not felt this satisfied in a long time, if ever. He spent much of the drive just thanking God for the way his and Tori's relationship was shaping up. Yep, God was moving—of that he was sure.

He parked the car and went around, opening Tori's door. "I love that you open doors for me. My dad is quite chivalrous as well. Thank you for living up to the standard he set that you didn't even know about." She giggled.

He bowed. "Glad it pleases you, fair maiden."

When he straightened, her face had turned white and a look of horror settled over her features.

"Tori, are you all right?" Jake turned to see what had captured her attention. Turned out it was not a what, but a who.

"Spense?" She spoke the name so softly that Jake barely heard it.

Spense barreled up to them, grabbed Tori around the waist, and laid a kiss on her that made Jake's seem like kid's play.

"What are you doing?" Tori asked when he let her up for air.

"I'm here, baby, because I made a big mistake. Big. I need your forgiveness." He went to his knees. "I'll beg if I need to."

Tori said nothing. He pulled a super-sized diamond from his pocket and slipped it on her finger. She wore a deer-in-the-headlights expression but didn't object.

Say something, Tori. Tell him to get lost. Tell him about me.

Say something. Jake suddenly felt like a voyeur. He took a step back.

Spense rose and swept Tori into his arms. Still no protest from her.

"Baby, we need some privacy." He glanced pointedly at Jake and carried her off into the sunset like some romantic movie, and she never said a word.

❧

Her head spun. His kiss brought back all the old feelings. *Am I over him? Do I still love him? What about Jake? I don't ever remember Spense kissing me like that or it affecting me like this.* A part of her heart that had died was just resuscitated.

She lay there in his arms like a helpless babe, reveling in his words of love, apology, even his willingness to beg. She glanced at her left hand lying limp across her stomach. The ring was back. He'd saved it for her. A part of him must have always known she was the one for him.

God, is this You finally answering all those prayers? Had God brought Spense back to her? Was this His will for her life?

She noticed people staring at them and felt silly being carried around by some big he-man. "Where are we going?"

"Your place." He headed up the staircase straight to her room. *How did he know where she lived?* So many questions shot through her brain at warp speed.

He set her down between him and the door. Was he afraid she'd attempt an escape? With a key he pulled from his pocket, he unlocked her door and carried her over the threshold, kicking the door closed with his foot. Then he carried her to the sofa, sitting with her on his lap.

He ran smooth manicured fingers across her cheek. "I love you, baby. I've never stopped. Thanks for forgiving me and taking back the ring."

Had she done those things? Did she forgive him or agree to take the ring back? Everything happened so quickly.

He kissed her again. Slow and easy. Like they didn't have a care in the world. "Tell me that you love me." The words sounded more like a demand than a request.

But she couldn't say the words. Nothing was resolved. Nothing had changed. And his appeal hit her like a bucket of cold water.

She pushed herself off his lap and crossed the floor to put distance between them. Her emotions reeled in twenty directions. Her heart pounded. What was she doing? She pushed her hair back out of her face, turning to gaze at her once beloved Mr. Tall, Dark, and Handsome. It was just like him to storm in here and tell her how she felt. He used his words well, manipulating by the way he strung each phrase together, leading people to believe it was their idea. She'd seen him do it before, and now he tried to do it to her. *Thanks for forgiving me and taking the ring back.* She'd done neither!

Placing her hands on her hips, suddenly angry—probably more at herself than at him, but he was on the receiving end. "How dare you assume you can march in here and sweep me off my feet! You think one kiss, one apology and I'm putty in your hands?"

He rose from the couch.

"Don't take a step toward me, not a step!"

He stopped and sat back down.

"I don't forgive you! I haven't forgiven you. And we are not engaged!" She jerked the ring off her finger and hurled it at him. She marched over to the front door and opened it, grabbing one of his suitcases and chucking it through the doorway. It landed with a bang in the hall.

This time Spense rose and grabbed her before suitcase number two flew out the door. "Are you nuts? Have you lost your mind?" He pried his expensive piece of black luggage from her hand and set it outside the door. He did the same with his computer case.

"You just need some time, Tori. I know you missed me. And your kiss tells me that you still love me. I was confused. I made the wrong choice. I'll be here a couple of weeks, so we have plenty of time to work through this. I love you, Tori. And you love me. True love conquers all. You'll see." He leaned down and kissed her cheek. "Dream about me tonight."

She held out her hand toward him. He grinned, pulled the ring from his pocket, and laid it in her open palm, looking like the cat who'd caught the mouse.

"I want my key."

He sheepishly pulled it from his pocket, laying it next to the ring.

"And do not ever break into my place again, or I'll have you arrested." She slid the key into her pocket and handed the diamond back. "I don't want this."

He plucked the ring from between her thumb and forefinger, probably afraid she'd hurl it at him again if he didn't act swiftly. She pointed toward the door, and he made his exit. She slammed the door behind him and leaned back against it. Wow, she'd never been that assertive before! It actually felt good not to let him push her around and to have her own opinion about something.

Taking a few deep breaths, she headed downstairs to the registration desk. No one was there but Mindy. "Did you give my ex a key to my room?" Her tone was more accusatory than she'd intended.

Mindy's eyes widened, and she nodded. "He didn't tell me he was your ex."

"I don't think that is good business practice to be so trusting. Please put a note in my computer file that I don't want anyone, not even the president of the United States, to have access to my room." Tori slipped the extra key across the counter.

Mindy grabbed it and typed something into the computer. "I've made note as you requested. And I apologize."

Tori caught sight of the fear in Mindy's eyes. "I'm not mad at you, but at him. I know how charming he can be."

Mindy smiled. "He can, can't he?"

"When it suits him. You had the key. He wanted it. He poured on the charm. You gave in. I've seen the scenario again and again. I've fallen for it more times than I care to admit. Have you seen Jake around?"

Mindy shook her head.

How must all this look to him? She needed to find him and try to explain. He'd been eyewitness to the kiss that should have been stopped by her, but wasn't. She went outside. His SUV was gone. He must have gone home for the night. She tried to call him when she got back to her room, but he didn't pick up. She tried several more times, but it always went straight to voice mail. He'd turned his phone off!

≈

Tori hadn't slept well. Jake must be mad or hurt or something. She tried to call him just before leaving for her office, but still no answer. This time she decided to say more than just, "Call me."

"Jake, I don't know what to say except I'm sorry. Spense and I are *not* back together, all is *not* forgiven, and I returned his ring. I know how it must have looked to you, but I think I was so shocked to see him that I couldn't respond. Please come by and see me at work today. Thanks. And please forgive me."

She shut her phone and headed to her office. It was weird living and working at the same place. Her office was just across the way, and it took about two minutes to get from home to work.

After signing on to her computer, she clicked her e-mail shortcut. An e-mail from Jake's secretary sent at seven this morning stated Jake had been called away suddenly and would be gone for two weeks. Tori wanted to cry. He must know Spense was here for two weeks, and he couldn't bear to see them together.

She and Jake might end up being the shortest-lived relationship in the history of man and woman.

As Tori alphabetized the purchase orders, she noticed another one for Jake for almost five hundred dollars. There had been one last week for the same amount. Something seemed amiss. Her stomach churned. She rose from her desk and went to the file cabinet. She pulled out the drawer containing the Ms and searched until she found the file labeled MATTHEWS, JAKE. She pulled the file from her drawer and returned to her desk.

Opening it, she discovered Jake turned in weekly reimbursements for several hundred dollars. The signatures were Jake's. The receipts included with each purchase order didn't support the amounts, but since he was the boss, apparently no one questioned him or asked for more accurate records. What did this mean? Was Jake stealing from the company?

Tori felt sick at the thought. She loosened the scarf

around her neck. Breathing was difficult. How could this be happening? She closed her eyes and prayed. "Please don't let this be as it seems." Were both the men she'd fallen for in her life scumbags?

Tori returned the Matthews file to its proper place. Then she slipped into the document storage area to check the bank statements. She pulled out all of the current year's information and carried it back to her desk. Along with the bank statement, a copy of each check was included. Tori searched for the ones made to Jake. All that was on the back on the endorsement line was a hand-scribbled *For deposit only.* She returned them to the document room and decided to take a walk. She needed some fresh air.

nine

Once outside and away from human ears, she called Jen. Between the suspected embezzlement and the Spense situation, she needed a friendly voice. One she knew she could trust—no matter what.

Jen answered. "Hey, aren't you supposed to be at work?"

"That's some greeting. What happened to hello?"

"The flaw of caller ID." Jen giggled. "Sorry. Hello, Tori. How are you?"

"That's better, and thanks for asking. I'm terrible. Spense is back." She'd circled the lodge once and started on round two.

"What?" The disbelief resounded in Jen's one-word answer.

"Yep. He showed up yesterday." Tori rounded the corner and waved at the men working on the ski lift.

"Showed up? Isn't he supposed to be honeymooning this week? Surely he didn't bring Bella?"

"No Bella—just him with my ring, which he used to reclaim me in the first ten seconds after arriving. And in front of Jake, no less, who is now MIA."

"Wait," Jen demanded. "I have to sit down to digest all this. TMI."

"You think it's too much information for you? How do you think I'm feeling?"

"Overwhelmed. What happened to Bella? Did he leave her at the altar?"

"I don't know. He hasn't mentioned her." Tori sat on a secluded bench where she could overlook Lake Pend Oreille.

"All I know is that he is here—no explanations or backstory."

"Are you engaged again?" Tori caught the "you'd be nuts" accusation in Jen's tone.

"No! I returned the ring—threw it at him actually." She felt a surge of empowerment, but embarrassment followed on its heels.

"You don't do things like that. Should I congratulate you or scold you?" Jen chuckled.

"Both. I did stand up for myself, which might be a first." She leaned back against the wrought-iron bench, willing her tight muscles to relax.

"A learning curve is involved, like with anything. It's a start. I'm proud of you. So where do things stand with the two—three—of you?"

"Jake is missing. We'd returned from an all-day outing with his friends, and Spense approached as we were just leaving the car." She filled in Jen on the incident.

"He kissed you, regained possession of your ring finger, and carried you off into the sunset without protest. I'm astounded. How did that happen?"

Tori shook her head, wondering that herself for the millionth time. "I've never felt so overwhelmed with emotion. The kiss brought back so much that I was reeling."

"Poor Jake. Sounds like he made a polite and quiet exit to give you space with Spense." Jen sucked in a deep breath. "Are you still in love with Spense?"

"I don't know. I'm confused. Is this the answer to all those prayers I prayed the first few months of this year? Did God bring Spense back? Is that His will for me?"

Jen sighed. "You'll have to spend some time in prayer to figure all that out. My gut reaction is no—God didn't bring Spense back. He's a two-timing jerk who wandered back of his own accord."

"Maybe God wants me to exercise grace." Tori rose and stretched her tight back.

"Tori, you have this great guy in Jake. Maybe the enemy wants to throw you off track. Remember when Pastor Roger spoke on God having a perfect will for our lives and Satan trying to trick us with a counterfeit? Please be careful." Tori could picture Jen's concerned expression.

"Well, Mr. Great Guy has slipped from his saddle. He's not who I thought." Tori filled her in on the bookkeeping scam that made Jake look pretty guilty.

"Nooo." Jen used her whiny tone. "Please tell me it's not true! I can't take this. Jake an embezzler?"

"Looks that way." Saying the words broke her heart. "What do I do?"

"Pray hard." That was always Jen's answer. She was a woman of strong faith. "Have you talked to maternity-leave girl? Maybe she has some answers that would clear up the whole mystery."

"How do I do that without incriminating Jake?"

"With innocent-sounding questions and a no-clue demeanor. Works all the time. Don't sound accusing—sound confused."

"Thanks, Jen. You never let me down."

"I try not to." Jen paused. "Tori, please be careful with Spense. I don't have a good feeling about him."

"I will, but remember, by your own admission, you never liked him. Maybe you can't have an unbiased opinion where he is concerned."

❧

"Jake!" Roni hugged him in the doorway before escorting him into their very sleek, modern living room. "Have a seat.

Tom," she said, raising her voice on the last word. "Jake's here."

Tom stepped down into the formal living room. Jake stood, and they did their ritualistic cousin handshake, ending with a hug and pat on the back.

"I had no idea you were coming to town." Tom settled into a low chair that sat diagonal to Jake's. Roni settled on the couch, curling her feet under her just the way Tori did.

Tori. . . He'd debated even coming here or letting them know he was in town. But since Tom was the brother he'd never had, he knew he had to man up and face the hard things. It would be less awkward if Tori weren't Roni's twin.

"Has Tori caught on to her job? Is she liking Idaho? She called a few days ago during dinner, so I couldn't talk. I should text her." Suddenly Roni stopped. "I'm sorry. Where are my manners? Would you like something to drink?"

"Water would be nice."

She glanced at Tom. He dutifully rose and headed for the kitchen.

"Tori caught on really quickly, and Idaho surprised her. You and Tom should visit. I think you'd be surprised, too, in a good way."

Tom returned with three waters in crystal glasses, a lemon floating in each.

Jake raised his brows. "You've been domesticated, buddy."

"Presentation." He glanced at Roni and smiled.

"It's everything," Roni chimed in.

"Well, how is this for presentation?" He retold the Spense story.

"No way! Tori can't be that dumb." Jake realized Roni's bluntness only fed Tori's insecurities.

"She's not dumb," Jake defended. "I don't think she's over

him." He ran a hand through his hair.

"I thought you two had hit it off." Tom leaned toward Jake.

"What? I had no idea." Roni's brows rose like an exclamation point above her face.

"Maybe you would if you took Tori's call once in a while," Tom reprimanded his wife gently.

"She calls at the worst possible times." Roni's voice had a defensive edge. "Tell me, Jake. I have a right to know. She *is* my sister."

"Which is the very reason I hesitate. I mean, it's her story to tell."

"It's your story, too, and you have every right to tell your cousin's wife."

"Always the lawyer." Jake laughed. He gave Roni a very short version of his and Tori's brief romance, leaving out the kisses, the depth, and the pain. He pulled his cell phone from his pocket. "She left me this message the night Spense hauled her away without a word of protest from her."

He hit the number one to retrieve his messages and put it on speaker so they could all listen. "Jake, I don't know what to say except I'm sorry. Spense and I are *not* back together, all is *not* forgiven, and I returned his ring. I know how it must have looked to you, but I think I was so shocked to see him that I couldn't respond. Please come by and see me at work today. Thanks. And please forgive me."

"That was Monday morning. I had several missed calls from her on Sunday evening."

"You have to believe her. Tori is nothing if not sincere." Roni's eyes pleaded her sister's case.

"I know that, but why didn't she fight back? Why didn't she say anything? He kissed her, put the ring on her finger, and carried her away. She never uttered a sound, never pushed him away. She did nothing! Nothing! What does that tell you? It tells me she's still in love with Spenser King!" Jake shook his head. His eyes bore into Roni. "What would you have done?"

Roni took her time mulling the question. "I'd like to tell you I'd have slapped that two-timing jerk across the face and told him to get lost, but who really knows what we'd each do in any given situation until we are in the midst of it?"

"A very sisterly answer." Jake couldn't hide his frustration.

"Give her a chance to explain," Roni encouraged.

He picked up his phone and hit number two on his keypad. Tori had been assigned the highest position in his speed dial. He counted the rings. Four. Five. Six. She didn't pick up. After the beep, he said, "Tori, it's me. Sorry I sat on your message a few days. I do want to understand, so call me."

Why did he think she'd be worth the risk? He knew she still grieved Spense, and he'd tried to rush her through the process. Now he faced additional heartbreak.

❧

Tori felt his presence before she actually saw Spense. She glanced up from her computer screen, and he greeted her with a smile. How like him to act like everything between them was resolved. Looking back, she saw a pattern of him sweeping things under the proverbial rug.

"I wondered when you'd show up."

"So you were waiting for me, weren't you?" He flashed that cocky grin of his and nodded. "You wanted me to come crawling. Well here I am, baby, crawling back to you. What do you say to dinner tonight?"

She wanted to say no. How had she missed his growing arrogance over the years? Now that he was a local Minnesota celeb, it had become almost unbearable. *But what if God brought him back to me?* "I will have dinner with you because I have some questions I still need answers to."

"Yes, I still love you. No, I never stopped. Yes, I'm sure you're the only one for me. Does that about cover those questions of yours?"

"Not even close. I'll meet you at the Blue Coyote at seven."

His grin indicated he was pleased with himself, and his chest almost visibly puffed out as he left her office.

Was he always that obnoxious? She didn't have time to ponder, though. All her detective work had put her behind on her actual job, so she returned her attention to the pile of tasks.

At seven Tori entered the restaurant that was actually housed in one end of the lodge where her tiny apartment sat. The maître d' led her to a table for two where Spense waited with a bouquet of white roses and lilies. The sight of her favorite flowers softened her heart a bit. He remembered.

Spense rose and kissed her cheek before pulling out her chair. She settled in, her eyes scanning the full room for coworkers or acquaintances. She saw no familiar faces. Letting out a sigh of relief, she accepted the menu Spense offered.

They spent a few minutes scanning the list of options before much was said. She knew Spense hated the waiter having to return more than once for the order, so she'd learned to make a decision before making small talk. After they placed their order, she swallowed a sip of water, studying the glass and sending up a prayer for wisdom and discernment.

She raised her eyes to meet his. A pang of regret hit her, and she could have easily cried, but refused. If only there'd been no Bella, they'd soon be saying "I do," but now they sat here in awkward silence. She wondered how to proceed, deciding on the direct approach—a new way for her to deal with things.

"I need to hear the Bella story from beginning to end." Her cell rang. She pulled it from her clutch and glanced at the screen. Jake! She couldn't talk to him now. She hit the ignore button.

"That fellow you were with the other night? Can't he take a hint or what?"

At her stare, Spense stopped talking, cleared his throat, and began the Bella story in a well-modulated tone. "As you know, my family loves Bella. They always have."

She nodded. "And none of them ever seemed to care much for me." She'd tried, but they were all so set on Bella being the next Mrs. King that they held Tori at arm's length.

He nodded. It was the first time he'd not denied the facts. That encouraged her. Maybe they were both changing for the better. "Bella was my first love, and I guess in some small way, that first love always owns a piece of your heart."

Boy did she know that to be true.

"We were together a long time. All the way through high school. Things happened between us that I never told you about."

Tori swallowed hard. "You had sex with her?"

He nodded, all the arrogance gone for the moment. "I'm not proud of that, Tori. She became overly possessive. I had to get away. She wanted to get married and have babies. I was barely eighteen. My mom was thrilled when I chose a Christian college. She'd been praying for me to grow for a long time. So I headed out and broke it off with Bella soon after arriving at school."

The waiter delivered their salads and filled their water glasses.

Spense waited until he was gone and continued in a low tone. "When you and I became engaged, everyone turned up the pressure. My mom cried. My dad shared his disappointment. My sister stopped speaking to me."

His words hurt. They cut deep. "All because you chose me instead of her?"

He nodded and slid his hand across the table to squeeze hers. He didn't let go, and she didn't pull away. The reassuring warmth of his hand redeemed some of the hurt at his family blatantly destroying their relationship.

"Bella moved to the city and got an apartment in my building. She invited me to dinner. I should have known better but said yes. Since I moved to the Twin Cities, I missed home-cooked meals. My mom kept my fridge stocked when I lived in their town. It had been months. . . ." He swallowed hard, and his eyes actually looked teary in the low lighting of the restaurant.

Her heart went out to him. He didn't actually dump her of his own free will. Maybe God was redeeming them after all and freeing him from a controlling and manipulating family. She tightened the grip on his hand. "Go on."

He also tightened his grip. "This next part will be hard for you to hear." His eyes held regret and apology.

She swallowed hard, fear creeping up her back like an unwelcomed guest.

"She answered the door in a sexy black cocktail dress. The lights were low. Candles on the table. Delicious smells floated at me from the kitchen. I stood on the threshold and debated. I wanted what she was offering. A voice in my head said run and reminded me of the years of celibacy. I could do it. I turned to walk away. She took my hand and pulled me inside." He paused.

Jealousy flowed through Tori's veins. She thought of the adulterous woman spoken about in Proverbs. Spense had been seduced and had fallen into Bella's well-laid trap.

"I thought just this once. Just one more time. Then I'll repent and get things right with God. I figured you'd never have to know." His head drooped in shame.

Her heart ached for him, for them. They'd been victimized.

"I gave in, but like a bug in a spider's web, I couldn't get out. Couldn't stop. My appetite for more sucked me deeper into the pit of sin."

"So it happened more than once?" Tori dreaded his answer.

He nodded. "I hated myself, but felt like the man Paul described in Romans 7. I did what I didn't want to do and didn't do what I wanted. Every time was going to be the last, only it never was. I'm sorry, Tori."

"Me, too." She blinked away the tears. "This explains the distance."

He nodded. "You unknowingly exacerbated the guilt and self-loathing. It was easier to avoid you."

"What finally brought you to the point of breaking our engagement?"

"Guilt. You deserved better. Family pressure. Bella announcing she was pregnant."

Tori shook her head. "You're going to be a dad?" The break in her heart cracked deeper.

"Excuse me." The waiter appeared. "Neither of you have touched your salads. Is there a problem with the food?"

"Just deep in conversation," Spense answered.

"I don't normally have the meal started until you're about halfway through the salads. What would you like me to do?"

He seemed perplexed as to proper protocol.

"I'm not hungry," Tori admitted. "I don't think I could force a bite down my throat."

"Since you haven't started our actual meal, can I just pay for the salads?"

"Yes, sir. I'll get your bill."

Tori excused herself and headed for the restroom. She locked herself in the stall and indulged in a few tears. She patted her face dry with a piece of toilet paper and stepped out of the stall. After repairing her makeup, she looked better, but there was no way to hide the red-ringed eyes. Upon exiting, she found Spense waiting at the door.

"I can't process anything else tonight." Forcing the words past the lump in her throat was nearly impossible. "I'm going to my room."

"Wait, Tori. I'll walk with you." He followed her toward the stairs that led to her place. "You have to know that I didn't walk out on Bella and a baby. She lost the baby a couple of weeks before he could sustain life on his own. I wouldn't have walked out on her if the little guy had lived."

"So you just walked out on her?" Sorrow nearly choked the breath out of Tori. She headed up the stairs without another word. Tears streamed from her eyes, but this time the tears weren't just for herself, but for Bella and a little boy who'd never be held in his mom's aching, empty arms.

ten

Saturday morning Tori headed to Allison's hospital room with a baby gift in tow. She followed the signs in the corridor to the correct room in the maternity wing. She still hadn't returned Jake's call from Thursday evening. After her dinner with Spense, her emotions were like a teeter-totter—up, down, and all around. She had nothing left to put into a conversation with Jake.

"Hey, Allison. Feel like company?" she asked, rounding the corner into the room. The baby girl lay nestled in her mommy's arms, nursing.

"Sure, come on in. Jim ran out to grab some lunch. Neither of us can get into the hospital food." Allison peaked under the blanket covering her and the baby.

"I won't stay long, I promise." Tori sat the gift bag with the cheerful yellow- and pink-spotted giraffe on the bedside table. "So, how are you? And how was the delivery?"

"Not bad. I'm going home later today and happy about that. Neither Jim nor I have slept well here. I had an epidural, so the delivery was uneventful. Would you like to hold her?" Allison offered.

Tori used the hand sanitizer and lifted the baby from her mother's arms. "What did you name her?"

"Hayleigh Rose. Rose is after my mother. How are things at work?"

"I'm so glad you asked. I did have a couple of procedural questions. I think that you told me on reimbursements that they had to be supported by receipts."

"That's correct. I suppose you're referring to Jake's receipts?"

Tori nodded. "His requests always have a couple of receipts, but they never come anywhere near supporting his claims."

Allison nodded, looking uncomfortable. "I know."

"So the rules are different for him?" Tori pulled her brows together.

"I guess." Allison shrugged.

"I checked with Rachel—because you said she did the job before you—and she said *every* claim must have documentation no matter who it's from. I asked if the higher-ups had an exemption to the rule, and she told me no." Tori shook her head back and forth to emphasize the no. "To quote her, 'Every person and every claim may only be reimbursed the amount of their receipts and not a penny more.'"

Allison squirmed, looking more uncomfortable all the time. "Chris told me to reimburse Jake, no matter what."

"Chris?" Had she met anyone named Chris?

"Jake's assistant. Chris Corbane. He was adamant. Told me that to do otherwise could jeopardize my job. I need my job. At the time Jim was in school, and I was our only source of income. I figured the assistant manager trumped Rachel, even though she was once in the position."

"So you've been doing Jake's reimbursements for years?"

"Four, ever since I started." Fear washed the color from Allison's face. "Am I going to be in trouble or get fired for this?"

"I don't think so, though you did disregard the policy."

Allison bit her bottom lip. "Because I was told to."

"Did you tell?"

"I never told anyone. Chris made me feel threatened if I didn't shut up and pay Jake's POs without question."

Did Jake involve Chris in this scheme somehow? Seemed to her that the fewer people who knew, the better.

"Are you going to report me?" Allison glanced at her baby in Tori's arms and started to cry.

Tori moved to Allison's side, placing a hand on her arm. "No, of course not. But what Jake is doing is illegal. Had you considered that?"

"Not really. I just didn't think about it at all. It was easier that way." She sniffed, dabbing her eyes with the sleeve of her hospital gown.

"I don't want Jim to know about this. He'll only worry. I carry the family insurance."

Tori carried the baby back to the chair in the corner while Allison washed her face and pulled herself together.

The baby wrapped her fingers around Tori's index finger. Soon Roni would have one of these, and Spense almost did. Tori held the bundle close and couldn't help but let her mind run to Bella. She felt sorry for her. Everything in her world had turned upside down, too.

After returning the baby to her mother, Tori followed the hall back the way she'd come. It was time to return Jake's call. Which man did she love? Which man was God's will? Maybe neither.

Once in her car, she pulled out her cell phone, scrolled down to his name, and hit TALK.

"Hello." Jake either didn't read his caller ID or was playing it cool.

"Hi, Jake, it's me." How she longed for the friend he once was. She wished she could confide in him about everything with Spense—and everything at work, for that matter.

"Hey, Tori." His voice sounded sad.

She wasn't sure how much more sadness she could take

without bawling her eyes out. She sat quietly on the phone with absolutely no idea what to say to him.

Finally, after several minutes of awkward silence, Jake spoke up. "I got your message last weekend."

"And I got yours on Thursday."

"So?" He apparently had no idea what to say either. "Were you with Spense when I called?"

Her stomach twisted into knots. "I was." She wanted to reassure him it wasn't what he thought, but she had no idea what it was. Or who Jake was. At least Spense came clean and admitted his wrongs. He seemed humble. Jake's whole life was a lie.

&

"You guys back together?" Jake's voice went higher than he'd planned. He'd hoped for a "no big deal" coolness, but fell far from achieving that.

"No." She offered nothing more than one tiny little word, made up of two lousy letters that told him nothing.

"Will you be by the end of next week when he leaves?"

Dead silence. He waited. Still nothing. Guess he had his answer.

"It's not that simple, Jake."

"Not that simple? I asked a yes or no question. About as simple as it comes." He didn't like being duped. It felt too much like a repeat of Kate. "Do you still love him?" The question demanded an honest answer.

"I don't know. I'm confused." She sniffled, and he was pretty certain she was crying.

"The way he treated you was awful. He doesn't deserve you."

"Perhaps you're right, but there were extenuating circumstances. Sometimes things aren't as they seem."

Jake saw the writing on the wall. This was not going to play out well for him. Did he bow out gracefully or fight for her? He decided on option two. "Tori, I love you. That hasn't changed."

She said nothing.

"I still want us to be together, but I'm really hurt. You let Spense come in, kiss you, and steal you away without a word."

"I apologized for that. He stunned me, and I couldn't think."

"Because his kiss meant something?"

"His was my very first real, grown-up kiss. He was my first everything—boyfriend, kiss, date, love, heartbreak. That kiss brought back a lot of emotion and memory. You just don't understand."

"No, Tori, I think the problem is that I understand far too well. You see, if Kate showed up out of the blue and laid one on me, I'd push her away because you're the only one I want to be kissing."

"You don't know that for sure. I'd have told you the same thing prior to last Sunday, but you can't possibly know what you'd do until you're in a situation."

"I do know." Anger laced his words. "And I also know you and Spense will be back together before he leaves the mountain next weekend. I should have known better than being your rebound guy. It never ends well."

"Even if I don't choose Spense, I could never choose you."

The words sliced deep. "And what is that supposed to mean?" He couldn't remember the last time he'd been this angry.

"It means you're not the man I thought you were," she accused.

"Oh, and Spense is? That's rich. You know what, Tori? Forget it. I'm through." She'd end it soon anyway. He might as well be the one to pull the plug and put them both out of their misery.

"You can't blame this on Spense, Jake. It has nothing to do with him and everything to do with you."

"Me? Last Sunday I was fine. Today I'm not worthy of you?"

"Whether or not Spense and I get back together, I would have ended it with you for a very separate and different reason."

"What are you talking about?" Jake threw his head back and slapped his forehead.

"You haven't been honest." She said the words in a quiet tone that he strained to hear.

"I haven't been honest? About what? You're the one who wasn't honest with me or yourself regarding Spense and being over him."

"I know that's how it must seem to you, but I was over him. Then I got over you and now I may try again with Spense, or I may not. Who knows?"

Jake sighed. "This conversation is pointless, but before we end it, I have to say it again. I was never in any way dishonest with you. I've never lied to you or misled you, contrary to whatever you think."

"You didn't lie to me. You live the lie, Jake. You have one persona but have a whole hidden life that I can't be a part of." She paused as if waiting for him to confess.

What in the world is she talking about?

"I'm hanging up now. Good-bye, Jake." There was a finality in her tone, and the call ended. Their romance also ended before it had ever really begun.

❧

Sunday morning Tori discovered a note had been slid under

her door. It caught her eye on the way to the bathroom. She recognized Spense's handwriting almost immediately. She'd always admired his bold writing style. Bending down, she picked the folded paper up off the floor and unfolded the note.

Tori,

  I'd like to join you for church, if you'd allow me. Then I hoped you'd spend the day with me in Sandpoint. Here is my cell number in case your answer is yes.

I'll always love you,
Spense

She held the note against her heart, asking God again if this was His plan for her life. Jake's face popped into her head. That couldn't be God. He'd not yoke her to a thief.

The note carried the slight scent of Spense. She breathed in deeply a few times, closing her eyes and savoring the closeness she felt again with him. After dialing his number, she placed the phone against her ear. *I probably should add his number to my contacts again.* He answered on the first ring.

"Tori! I hoped you'd call. Thank you." She'd never seen such humility from Spense.

She smiled. "And I did. I'd love for you to join me for church." She told him what time to meet her at the bottom of the stairs. After getting ready, Spense drove them down the mountain in his rented convertible. Whenever she was with Spense, heads turned. He was a good-looking man, and she'd always felt honored to be his chosen woman. Today proved to be no different. After the service, people went out of their way to speak to them.

As she faded into the background and in light of the

sermon, she couldn't help but think about Jake. She'd been hard on him yesterday. And today she did have regrets. Yet she was grateful to the Lord for revealing his embezzling ways; otherwise, she might have married the guy without ever knowing. The Lord was protecting and guiding her. Without Jake as a contender, the idea of returning to Spense was much more palatable.

"You ready?" Spense shined his fourteen-karat smile on her.

At her nod, Spense reached for her hand. If anyone had noticed her last week, she left this same building walking hand in hand with another man. Somehow the thought made her feel cheap. She pulled her hand from Spense's, digging through her purse for lip gloss to make the action look natural and not like rejection.

Spense also treated a lady like a lady. That was about the only similarity between him and Jake. He held open the car door and waited until she got the full skirt of her dress out of the doorway and tucked around her ankles. He bent down and placed a peck on her mouth. "I love you. Always have. Always will." He shut her door and didn't seem to expect a response.

Did he use the same phrase with Bella? Tori couldn't help but wonder.

As they drove toward Ivar's, Spense's chosen lunch destination, Tori asked, "Why did you tell me that you'd never loved me at the breakup scene?"

"I don't know." He glanced her direction and shifted the car. "I thought it would make it easier somehow."

"For who? You or me?"

"Selfishly, me. For a while I convinced myself I had never loved you. That made what I was doing with Bella more bearable."

"Did you tell her that you loved her?"

He parked the car. "Do we have to relive this again?"

"I do. Did you?"

He turned off the engine. "I did and do love Bella. I'm just not *in* love with her."

"What does that even mean?" She hated the way he played with words.

"It means that you're the one I want to spend the rest of my life with." He reached for her hand.

"Why did you show up here in such arrogant style last Sunday?"

He pulled his hand away and ran it through his hair. "The truth is that I hoped not to have to delve into all this. I'd hoped you'd forgive me and we'd just move on."

"Just a little more dirt under our rug?" Her sudden anger seeped into the accusation.

He shrugged. This wasn't the first time she'd accused him of not dealing with their problems.

"If I'd have welcomed you back with open arms, we'd not have had the Bella discussion. Is that what you're saying?" It was more of a statement than a question.

He shrugged. "Maybe someday. Anyway, it doesn't matter because God made me face and confess the whole thing."

But it mattered to her. His transparency had been a ploy to gain her sympathy. If his strategy had worked, the truth may never have been told. The rest of their day was spoiled for her.

❧

"Hey, Tori." She glanced up from her computer screen on Monday morning, and there stood Chris, purchase order in hand. "Can you give this priority status?"

"Sure." She shot her sweetest smile his direction. Taking

the PO and quickly adding the receipts, she hollered, "Hey, Chris," just as he turned into the hall.

He popped his head back into her office.

"I'm a little confused." She wrinkled her forehead.

"About what?" His impatience showed.

"Two things actually. The receipts only come to $92.50, but the amount on the purchase order is $342.50."

He shrugged. "So? It's Jake. No big deal. Just pay it." He spun around to leave.

"Wait, Chris. You know I'm new here and was told to only pay the receipts that are turned in. I don't want to break the rules."

"Tell you what." Chris stepped into her office, closing the door behind him.

Tori's heart pounded. Was she in any sort of danger? Her mouth went dry.

"You'll be breaking Jake Matthews' rules by not complying, and that is a lot more serious than the accounting rules. You get my drift?"

She gave him a wide-eyed nod. "Would you initial it for me? That way I'm covered?"

She had the feeling he'd like to cuss her out, but he grabbed a pen from her desk caddy and initialed the amount. As he turned to leave, she spoke up again.

"Remember, I have two questions and haven't asked the second?"

He glanced at his watch. "I'm running late. Is this really necessary?"

"No." She shook her head. "You go ahead. I'll pose my second question to Rachel." Again, she put on her wide-eyed innocent expression. The one she and Roni had used a few times to coax Dad into giving them their way.

"I have time."

I thought you might.

"But please hurry." He again checked his watch.

"Isn't Mr. Matthews out of town?" She puckered her brow to reinforce her state of confusion.

"Yes, why?"

"Who signed his name on the purchase order?"

"He did before he left. Is that all Miss—?"

"Wade. Miss Wade, but call me Tori. Jake does." She rather enjoyed this game of cat and mouse with him. He squirmed at her last statement.

"Fine, Tori it is. Now if you'll excuse me." Once more he made a beeline for the door.

"Wait. I still haven't asked my question. How can he have signed it when it came off the printer less than an hour ago? He's been gone for a week." She used her dumbed-down voice but pointed out the time stamp on the document.

"I signed it, okay? I sign stuff for him all the time—with his permission of course."

"Of course." She stared at the signature. "You do a really good job. Good thing you're a nice man because I think you could get into forgery, if you had a mind to." She gave him another syrupy smile and batted her lashes.

"Good thing. Now I must run." He headed out the door like a man rushing to a fire or from one.

Tori let out a sigh. Maybe it wasn't Jake. Maybe it was Chris. Either that or they were in cahoots. She dialed Jake's cell phone. She'd know in a minute.

"Matthews here." He'd know by the caller ID that it was someone from work, but he'd not know who.

"It's Tori."

"Tori!" Surprise filled his voice. "Everything okay?"

"Yes. Just a quick question. I have a PO to reimburse you for a few items, but someone else signed your name because I know you're not here to do so. Should I pay it?"

"Yes. Give the check to Chris as usual."

Her heart dropped. He was in on it. "But I feel a little funny about it. The receipts don't add up to the total, and the strangest thing is the receipts are dated for this past week. You weren't even here." She continued with the confused, dumb-girl routine, which would get her further than accusations would.

"Tori, just pay the thing and don't ask so many questions." Impatience laced each word.

"I just want to do my job well," she assured him.

"And you are. I'll get the receipts straightened out when I get back. In the meantime, please just do what's asked of you. Print the check so Chris can deposit it for me."

"Will do. Thanks for your time." How disappointing. For a brief minute, she'd hoped for another culprit other than Jake. "Bye." She laid the phone in its cradle and teared up. Was there a man alive who was worth loving?

eleven

"Jen, you will not believe my day." Tori sighed.

"We haven't talked in a few days. I need lots of updating." Jen's honest voice sounded so wonderful to Tori.

"First, I need your advice about a work situation. Then I'll fill you in on the mess that is my life." Tori curled her pajama-clad body up on one end of her sofa.

"Ready, willing, and listening," Jen assured her.

"I think Jake is an embezzler." She blurted the words out. How could she soften them? Truth was truth.

"What? No way. I've met him. He's so sincere, kind, honest. You've got to be wrong on this one."

"You are echoing my own thoughts before I arrived here to work. I would have bet my life on that man, but do we really know anyone—the deep and apparently dark insides of people? I don't think so." The words ended on a hopeless, defeated note. "I could have married him and watched as my husband was shipped off to jail. My children could have been prison orphans."

"Are you sure? Absolutely, one-hundred-percent positive? Because you are making pretty big allegations."

"Don't I know it?" Tori rubbed her forehead. The tension had been mounting all day. Now the ache felt strong enough to split her head in half.

"Start at the beginning. Tell me the whole story with every detail you can remember—even the seemingly insignificant ones."

Tori did as Jen asked, finishing the story with today's events. "What do I do?"

"At the very least, you turn in your two weeks' notice and hightail it out of there before you get some accessory charges stuck to your name and hauled off to jail yourself."

"Could that really happen, or do you watch too much TV?" Tori had to admit the same thought had crossed her mind. Did knowing and not acting equal aiding and assisting? Fear lodged itself in the pit of her stomach.

"I honestly don't know, but it isn't worth the risk."

"So you think I should quit."

"Yes. Absolutely. Turn in your notice tomorrow."

"Do I turn him in?"

"You've got to figure that out with God, girl. I don't even know what to tell you."

"I don't want to," Tori admitted. Jake's sweet face popped into her memory.

"Are you afraid?" Jen questioned.

"Not of Jake. Maybe a little of Chris."

"What are you feeling for Jake these days?"

"Well, I've done a lot of sorting through things the last few days. The only thing I know for sure is my emotions are way over the top. I really like so many things about Jake, but can't be involved with him. He's breaking the law."

"And Spense?" Jen questioned.

"Spense is still Spense. I saw signs of change, but yesterday I spotted glaring reminders that the changes may have been more of an effort to win me back than actual change." Tori told Jen all about the heart-to-heart she and Spense had last week. "He was vulnerable, honest, even transparent, and though what he shared was extremely painful for me to hear, it felt possible to forgive him and move forward together."

"Then yesterday happened with all the glaring reminders?" Jen was such a good listener. She never missed a thing.

"Now I realize I don't want to marry a man who's already had a torrid affair behind my back. Not much to build a marriage on. Then I think about grace and how much God has bestowed on me. I mean, I've been stuck in fear forever, so I sort of understand what he means by getting stuck and wanting to stop, but not being able to."

"Tori, there is a huge difference between fear and sexual sin."

"I know, but I wonder. . .is there to God? Or is sin sin in His eyes—no matter what?" Tori had way more questions than answers at this point.

"I think it's the heart that matters to God. Once the sin is there, He wants it dealt with."

"And it's Spense's heart that I worry about. He still wants to sweep away his problems instead of acknowledging them." Tori glanced at her caller ID. "Hey, my mom is beeping on the other line, so I'll let you go."

"I'll be praying. You pray, too, and resign tomorrow. Love you, friend—" She heard Jen's parting words as she hit the TALK button to flip over to her mom.

"Hey, Mom," Tori greeted.

"And Dad." His voice sounded distant. They must have her on speakerphone.

"And Roni."

"And Tom."

"Wow, the whole gang's there!" She attempted to sound upbeat.

"How are you, honey?" Tori recognized the concern in her mom's voice. "We haven't heard much from you since you got there."

Guilt raised its ugly head. "Sorry, Mom. You're right. I haven't been good about calling. I did leave you a couple of messages, however. Did you get those?" Tori intentionally called when she knew they wouldn't be home. She wasn't ready to share this mess that was her life.

"I did," her mom admitted.

She put on her most cheerful tone. "So, how is everybody? How's the baby, Roni?" If she could get Roni going on herself, Tori would have to talk very little.

"We're all fine. I'm almost through my first trimester, which is a huge milestone. Tom and I had Jake show up at our house the other night." Roni took the bait but steered the conversation straight back to Tori. "We had the most interesting conversation."

They know that Spense is back. "Really?" *So Jake's in Arizona.* She hadn't been sure. *Did he mention his embezzling to you?*

"Tori, we're all concerned about you." Her dad spoke up for the first time during the conversation.

"Very concerned." Her mom parroted her dad.

"We understand Spense is back on the scene." Roni jumped into the mix.

"That he is." She pursed her lips, supplying no information. Whatever they wanted to know, they'd have to drag out of her.

"Are you and he. . .?" Her mom couldn't bring herself to finish the sentence.

"Back together? No, right now we're in limbo."

"Limbo? What does that mean?" Roni demanded.

"You know. Figuring things out." Tori's voice held a defensive edge.

"What's to figure out?" her dad asked. "The man broke your heart. There's nothing left to be figured out."

"Dad, has Mom ever hurt you?" Tori sighed.

"Nothing like what Spense did to you," her dad assured her.

"I don't think he should be trusted, Tori." Her mom strived for diplomacy.

The words rang with truth. Could she ever trust him? Every time he was late arriving home from work would she wonder if he'd been with another woman?

"Were you even going to tell us about him or about Jake?" Roni asked.

Oh great. Bag of worms number two.

"About Jake? What about Jake?" her mom questioned.

Deciding she'd rather put her own spin on it, Tori jumped in. "Jake and I were sort of starting to see each other."

"Until Spense showed up," Roni said.

"Now he's a nice boy." Her mom had suggested at the wedding that she consider him, but it had been way too soon for her to think about anyone.

"Yeah," her dad agreed. "He seems honorable."

"Meaning Spense isn't." Roni pointed out what their dad left unsaid.

"Thanks, Sherlock." Sarcasm dripped from Tori's statement.

"Girls!" Their mom hated when they skirmished.

"I really do appreciate all your concern, but Jake isn't everything you might think. Sorry, Tom."

"It's okay. None of us are."

"And Spense," she continued, "probably isn't as bad as you each think."

"What he did to you was horrible." Tori heard the disappointment in her mom's voice.

"Atrocious." Roni loved high drama.

"How many men have you broken up with? Seems like the pot calling the kettle names to me. He regrets the breakup and his cold feet."

"Cold feet? He dumped you for another woman. A far worse scenario than a pair of cold feet. Then he proceeded to dump her and is hoping to rekindle things with you. I never behaved that way. And as you love reminding me, until Tom there was no long-term romance on my resume. No broken engagements. He's abandoned two people on their way to the altar. Two, Tori. Do you want to be the first and the third?"

She could never outargue her sister—the queen of debate. She got paid to do it and did it well. And the truth was, the more Tori had thought about what he did to Bella, the less likely she could ever begin again with him, but it was a matter of principle here. Her family had gotten too used to never-rock-the-boat, way-too-compliant Tori. It was her life after all. She didn't call them up and tell them their next move. *Maybe because they aren't about to do something really stupid.* Doggone her conscience anyway!

❧

"Matthews here."

"Jake, Tori." She sounded matter-of-fact.

"Did you pay that PO for Chris?" Concern wove its way through each word.

"Yes." She sounded surprised he asked. Surprised and suspicious.

"Is there another problem then?" He changed the subject.

"Jake. . . I. . . I wanted to thank you for offering me this summer job."

Where was this conversation headed? "But?"

Her sigh—loud and long—echoed through the phone line. "I find myself in a position where I must resign."

"Really? You heading back to Minnesota with the boyfriend?" Jealousy curdled his stomach, but he refused to let her know.

"He's not my boyfriend. And no, I'm headed back to Arizona."

"I need it in writing. Do you plan to give me two weeks or leave me high and dry?" The annoyance he felt came through loud and clear.

"I have a letter all typed and ready to go. I just wanted to let you know first. I thought it only fair."

You thought it only fair? He wanted to laugh. "Do you mind if I ask why you can't finish out the timeframe you originally agreed to?" He tried to fight the frustration he was feeling, but he wasn't succeeding.

"Just some things going on here that I can't be a party to. It's morally and ethically impossible for me to remain in my current job."

She knows. Her reference the other day to my dishonest lifestyle, added to her call about the PO. She knows. I was afraid of that. Tori is too smart for her own good and right now for my own good as well. Question is, did she tip Chris off? Would he hurt her? Jake couldn't be sure he wouldn't. He had to get back there ASAP or get her out.

"Tori, not everything is as it seems." He couldn't say more than that without possibly putting her in harm's way or without breaking his word.

She laughed a bitter sound. "Don't I know that! First Spense and now you. Men aren't as they seem, except for my dad. He is the real deal."

"So am I, Tori. So am I. Maybe someday you'll believe that about me. When will you head out?"

"Two weeks."

"Thanks for letting me know. I need to make a couple of calls. I might be able to release you sooner."

"Sooner?"

"Yeah, if you're unhappy, it might be best if you don't linger. One disgruntled employee can spoil it for everyone. I'll make a few calls. Why don't you plan on driving back tomorrow morning?"

"Tomorrow?" Her tone now held surprise and maybe a little disappointment. "That soon? I at least wanted to be honorable and stay for two weeks."

"Tori, honorable would be seeing our contracted time period through to the end. I think it best if you leave in the morning. I'll make arrangements for a temp or someone to cover your remaining shifts."

"That will be fine." She swallowed hard, the sound echoing across the miles.

"I will need you to be out of your room by noon. That way I can offer it to the temp for tomorrow night."

"Okay." An uncomfortable silence ensued. "So is this good-bye?"

"Guess it is. I'm sure we'll see each other on occasion at family functions. Safe travels, Tori."

"Bye, Jake." The two words echoed in finality.

He knew getting her out was the right thing, even if it cost him the relationship. Maybe someday he could explain everything, she could forgive him, and they could try again. Or maybe she'd move to Minnesota and they'd never see each other again.

He called his admin assistant and had her arrange for a temp starting tomorrow morning. Bless her heart, she never asked questions, never participated in office gossip, and never repeated anything she heard from anyone. She was worth her weight in gold.

twelve

"I'm leaving tomorrow for Arizona," Tori told Spense as they followed the host to a table for dinner that evening.

"What? I don't want to be here five more days without you. Rent a room, and let's play tourist together. How does parasailing sound?" His charcoal eyes sparkled with enthusiasm.

"You know I'm a chicken at heart," she reminded him as he pulled out her chair for her.

"Not nearly as big of one as you portray. Coming here was a gutsy move." He settled in the seat to her left.

"Maybe." She picked up her menu and then looked around it. "No, coming here was a cowardly way to deal with Roni's marriage and honeymoon pregnancy."

"Whoa. I'm behind on the news." He laid his menu down. "You ready to order? Here comes the guy from the other night."

Sure enough, the same waiter showed up at their table. "You two again?"

Tori laughed. "I heard an unspoken, '*Not* you two again!'"

"No, no, not at all. Welcome back. I hope you stick around long enough to enjoy some great food."

They both laughed. Spense assured him they wouldn't bail out early this time.

After ordering, Tori realized this was one of the lightest times she'd had in a week and a half. Life suddenly got heavy when Spense showed up. Somehow he had a way of stirring up havoc in her life.

"Tonight we're living it up. I owe you that much—a nice night on the town."

"You know, I think you're right, so nothing heavy tonight as far as conversation."

"Here, here." He clanged his water glass against hers.

"To us as friends." She smiled at Spense, letting him know how it would be.

He nodded. "To old friends and dear friends. 'A lifetime's not too long to live as friends.'" He quoted an old Michael W. Smith song.

The waiter brought their sampler appetizer. Tori helped herself to a fried zucchini slice.

"Do you mind if we pray first?"

She turned a shocked expression on him. "You want to pray in public?"

He nodded. "I'm working hard at being real with God and with people."

After he prayed, she asked, "This isn't for my benefit, is it?"

He faked offense. "You think I would do something like that?"

"Think?" She shook her head. "Know. Absolutely."

"I wish I would have met you now instead back in my jerk phase. Maybe I'd have stood a chance."

"You weren't a jerk when I met you. You were a sweet college guy with a heart of gold."

"That's who you saw, but not who I was. I was a jerk who used a girl for four years and dumped her for a chance at something better." He cut into his potato skin.

She liked this new Spense. "Why not go home and marry that girl? Not because you have to, but because you want to."

Spense finished chewing and seemed to contemplate his

answer. "I'm not sure she'd have me now." He shook his head, and a sad expression settled over his features.

"Boy, you sure burn a lot of bridges." She only half joked.

"Losing the baby felt like my ticket to run. And I did. I left Bella drowning in grief and in more pain than one human being should ever endure." He choked up over his own tactless behavior. "My parents aren't speaking to me, and neither is she."

"Why did you do that?" Tori slid her appetizer plate toward the center of the table.

"Look at all this food. And you're done?" Spense pointed to the food-laden platter.

"I'm saving room for my meal, and stop changing the subject. Why did you run from Bella?"

"I resented her. She trapped me on purpose, and without the baby, there seemed no reason to stay."

Tori's heart ached for Bella, and realizing that shocked her. "Spense, you've made a royal mess of your love life."

"Thanks for not hating me, Tori."

"You didn't get off that easy. I did for a while."

"And now?" Was he fishing?

"Just mild disgust." She smiled, and they both laughed.

The waiter brought their salads and took away the appetizer.

"You need to make things right with Bella." Tori let her gaze rest on his eyes and realized she was trying to reconnect him to the woman who'd destroyed their relationship. *I really am over him.* Her heart felt light and free, at least in regard to Spense. Jake was another story.

"That means there's no hope for us?" She heard the longing in his voice.

"I don't think so. I've moved on and so have you. You don't

want me back. It's the easy way out, but not the right way."

He reached for her hand, held it a moment, and stroked it tenderly with his thumb. "How'd you get so wise?" His tender smile warmed her heart. "Thanks for forgiving me. I'm sorry I came off like a cocky jerk in the beginning. Did I ruin things between you and Jake?"

Tori smiled. "You know, I really have forgiven you." The news surprised her, but she felt the peace. Even when they talked about Bella tonight, none of the normal jealousy stabbed at her heart. "It actually feels good. As for Jake, we wouldn't have survived the summer. I think your appearance only sped up the inevitable."

The waiter brought their main courses. As they ate, Tori updated Spense on her family and her struggles regarding Roni and feeling cheated. By the end of her story, they'd finished their dinner, and Spense insisted on ordering dessert. Once he'd done that, he turned to her.

"Another apology I owe you." He was truly pained by his treatment of her. But what he did to Bella was much, much worse.

She shook her head. "You've apologized enough to me for one lifetime. Make it a blanket statement to cover every crime for the past decade, and let's forget it."

"You have a good heart, Tori Wade. Will you stick around a few days longer?"

She wanted to. More to see Jake than to spend time with Spense—however, the thought of hanging out with him and catching up on old friends did sound appealing. But her sensible side kicked in. "I can't afford this place. Besides, I've got to get home and see if Roni's firm still needs a temp to catch up on filing. Otherwise it will be a long and broke winter."

"Let me treat you to your own private room for the next three days. You can travel on Saturday and Sunday, arriving back in Tucson to go to work on Monday morning. It's the least I can do."

Deep down inside she agreed with him. Besides, Jake should be back by then. She wanted one last chance to make things right between them. Not back where they were, but simply peaceful so that when they ran into each other at some future Nelson event, it wouldn't be uncomfortable for them or those around them.

Jake—her biggest regret on this trip. She'd hurt and betrayed him by not shutting Spense down. But in light of his business practices, it might not matter. Maybe that was God's protection over her. She had to stop thinking. It wouldn't change the facts. For a brief couple of days, she had two men vying for her; now she had none.

"A lot of emotions crossed that face of yours. This is a string-free offer. You don't even have to hang out with me if you don't want to."

"It's not that."

"Jake?"

She nodded. "There's just a lot going on."

❧

After dinner she agreed to Spense's plan. He headed back to the registration area to secure a room for Tori, starting tomorrow for three nights. Tori headed back to her office to do a little more digging. She unlocked the finance area then locked the door behind her. She wanted to find out when this skimming started and photocopy all the evidence. She worked tirelessly for several hours. When she slipped out of the office near midnight, her arms were laden with a large stack of copied purchase orders.

Once in her room, she pulled an empty suitcase from the closet and laid all the evidence inside. Then on a whim, she pulled her cell phone from her purse to call Jen. Glancing at the time—eleven fifty-two—she decided to go ahead and push button number three for speed dial. Jen rarely hit the sack before midnight.

"Hey, you. I mean, hello, Tori." She remembered their last conversation. "What's up?"

"I'm homeless and jobless. All in one fell swoop."

"Wow." Jen yawned.

Concerned, Tori asked, "Did I wake you?"

"Nope. I was reading and just started getting groggy." Jen yawned again and then laughed. "Sorry. So you resigned."

"Yeah, and he forced my hand. Wants me gone tomorrow." Tori began methodically packing the clothes from her dresser in the largest suitcase. She laid aside whatever she might need for the next few days.

"Why wouldn't he want the two weeks?"

"I think he knows I know about his financial malpractice and wants me out of his hair. And sooner is better. He practically insisted I leave tomorrow. Need my room for the next girl."

"What are you going to do?" Jen sounded wide awake now.

"I'm packing. Spense is putting me up for a few nights."

"What?" Jen nearly yelled.

"Nothing clandestine." She explained their agreement. "I agreed because I wanted to see Jake one more time. I'm going to confront him."

"Is that a safe and/or sane idea? People can do crazy things if they feel threatened."

"I really feel like I have to. I made copies of all the incriminating evidence."

"Why don't you go to the authorities? Why put yourself in harm's way? It's not worth the risk." Jen feared for her.

"I need him to know that I didn't choose Spense and would have chosen him, except for this one tiny life-altering detail."

"Why? Go visit him in jail after the fact."

"I'm praying he'll turn himself in."

"Do you think he will?" Tori pictured the doubt on Jen's face right about now.

"I hope so. I want him to be honorable and broken, but quite honestly, only God can do that work in his heart."

"What if your plan goes south? What if he isn't willing to turn himself in? Then what, Tori? He kills you and buries you in the mountain, and none of us ever see or hear from you again?"

"Somehow I know I'm not in danger. I know it with my whole heart."

"You can't know that for sure!" Frustration echoed across the miles. "If not Jake, maybe that Chris guy. You don't know him or what he's capable of."

"Jake won't let him hurt me." She knew that she knew. Then she thought about Spense and realized what a bad judge of character she was. How arrogant to think Jake had her back!

"You're right. I have no idea what I'm getting myself into." She stopped packing and sat on the bed. She buried her face in her hands. "I don't know what to do. Maybe I should just leave tomorrow and anonymously mail my evidence to the police."

"That's my vote. Did you figure out when this started and about how much money is involved?"

"It started a little more than four years ago, when they

hired Allison. I'm wondering if they somehow chose her, realizing her timid personality would cave easily under just a small amount of pressure. And she did. During that time they've taken around twenty-seven thousand dollars. Not a lot, but enough for jail time." The thought of Jake in jail broke her heart. How had she fallen in love with a thief?

❧

Thursday evening Tori agreed to meet Spense for dinner at eight o'clock. They'd spent the day sailing around Lake Pend Oreille. As she showered and got ready, she thought of the past two days with Spense. All day Wednesday they visited shop after little shop in Sandpoint. Neither purchased anything, but it was fun just to look. They talked about a million things, and tonight she felt homesick for him, knowing this was their last evening to be together—ever. Tomorrow she'd hang out at the lodge all day, hoping to run into Jake. Rumor had it he'd be back by then. Spense had arranged to spend the day water-skiing. Then he'd drive into Spokane and spend the night there, flying out Saturday morning.

Spense waited at a quiet table for two when she arrived. She wore a bright, breezy sundress and knew it complemented her sun-kissed skin, thanks to the day at the lake. He rose at her approach and pulled out her chair. "You look especially lovely tonight."

She smiled. "Thank you. And you, sir, are quite handsome." Nostalgia tugged at her heartstrings. If-onlys danced through her head, making her wish their lives had turned out differently, making her dream of a time before Bella when life with Spense was as carefree as sailing around a lake for hours on end.

Tears lingered near the surface. She had to stop reminiscing.

Picking up the menu, she scanned it, but nothing tempted her. Tonight she'd say a final farewell to Spense, and tomorrow she'd do the same with Jake. She'd miss what she and Spense once shared, and she'd miss what she and Jake almost had. Heading back to Arizona alone would be a painful reminder of not one, but two failed relationships.

"You seem rather pensive this evening." He laid his hand over hers.

Tears pooled in her eyes, and they felt as water-laden as the lake they'd sailed around earlier today. She smiled and swallowed but knew there was no way she could speak.

"You could come with me." He raised her hand to his lips, kissing it. "This doesn't have to be good-bye. Let's make it hello instead. Hello to a second chance, redeemed love, and new hope."

The waiter arrived. Thank heaven this time they had someone different than their past two visits. Spense ordered first while she scanned the menu and took a moment to pull herself together.

"I think I'll go light tonight with a salad and an iced tea."

"This doesn't have to be it," Spense said as soon as the waiter departed. "I love you and would like nothing more than to put this back on your finger." He reached into his pocket and pulled out the ring. "Say yes, Tori. Say yes, and I'm yours from this day on." His charcoal eyes pleaded with her. Spense took her other hand. "Me and you forever—just like we once planned."

"I can't." His offer was no longer even tempting, reinforcing the fact that she was so over him.

He let go of her hand and returned the ring to his pocket. Regret and sadness settled on his features.

This time she reached for his hand. "I love you, Spense,

and to quote you, 'but I'm not in love with you.'"

"And to quote you, 'What does that even mean?'" He bedazzled her with his smile.

The waiter dropped off her iced tea and refilled Spense's water. He also set a basket of bread in the center of the table.

"I didn't get it then, but I do now. I love the memory of you, the years of our lives that intersected, and the friendship that ensued. But I don't love you the way I once did." She took a roll from the basket.

"I wish I'd listened to my conscience that night and turned and run." He also grabbed a roll, cut it in half, and buttered it. "Life would have turned out a lot differently for both of us."

She realized that though that was true, she and Jake were much better suited for each other. And she'd never have known that without Spense's indiscretion. And maybe someday the Lord would bring another man who'd suit her even more perfectly.

They ate in silence. She picked at her salad, but it barely looked touched when the waiter carried it off. After paying the bill, Spense walked her to the bottom of her staircase. They stopped and faced each other.

"You sure I can't change your mind?"

She nodded. "I'm sure."

He pulled her into a tight hug. "This is it, isn't it? Sometimes a lifetime is too long to live as friends."

"Sometimes it is. Our season's over." She raised her head from his chest and looked deep into his eyes.

੩

Jake stepped off the elevator and his eyes caught sight of a couple hugging at the bottom of the staircase. Wait. Tori? Tori and Spense? Why was she still here? Why hadn't she left on Wednesday like he asked?

He couldn't pull his gaze from them. She leaned back from the hug and looked into Spense's eyes. He placed his hands on each side of her face. She nodded. He bent and whispered something near her ear. She stood on tiptoe, placing a sweet kiss on his cheek. Then turned and headed up the stairs. On her way up, she glanced back twice. The second time, Jake spotted tears glistening in her eyes. Well, if there'd been any question before, he had his answer now. Tori chose Spense. Not that Jake gave her any reason to choose him.

When Tori disappeared from sight, Spense turned and spotted Jake. He gave a slight nod that Jake returned and headed across the walkway to the condo he'd rented.

Jake went behind the reservation desk, annoyed that Tori hadn't given up the room as he'd requested.

Relief washed over Mindy's face when he showed up. "Can you cover for me for a quick sec?"

"Sure." Gave him a chance to snoop in privacy.

He typed in her name, but nothing came up. He typed in her room number, but someone else's name came up. Then he typed in Spense's name. Two rooms came up—the condo and a room in the lodge near the original one she'd been in. So Spense rented a room for her, and she stayed on a few extra days. That shouldn't bug him, but it did.

"Jake!"

Glancing up from the computer, Tori stood before him at the counter.

"You're still here." He stated the obvious, hoping his annoyance hit her in full force.

"Yep, but I did check out of the room as you requested, and I wanted to see when my new check-out time was."

"Eleven. Same as everyone else." He didn't even try to fight the rudeness.

"No, I'm sorry, but that wasn't what I meant. This will sound funny, but how long am I staying?"

"You don't know?"

She shook her head.

Jake typed in her name, knowing full well it would not come up in the computer. "You aren't even listed as a guest. Perhaps the room is under another name?" Sarcasm dripped from the question.

"Perhaps." She gave him the look—the one that says, *Enough!* "Try Spenser King."

"Yep. That is, unless he has someone else he's housing here as well." The comment was intended to dig. After all, Jake knew about Bella. Why didn't Tori seem to remember all the pain Spense caused her? Why would she expose herself to that all over again?

"Tonight's his last night in the condo. The room in the lodge is paid through Saturday morning."

"Thank you." She hesitated. "Are you busy all day tomorrow?"

"I'll be in my office most of the day. I've got things to catch up on. Why?"

"I hoped we could talk before I drive out on Saturday."

He studied her sincere face. "Seems to me there's not much to say."

"Just one more thing. Then I'll be out of your hair forever."

Was that what he really wanted? Didn't matter. She'd chosen, and it wasn't him.

"Jake, I stuck around three extra days just so you and I could meet and clear some things up." Her gaze pleaded with him to be kind and understanding.

"I really thought you'd be gone."

"Thought or hoped?" she asked point-blank.

"Thought."

He typed in his info and pulled up his Outlook calendar on the computer. "I don't have anything scheduled tomorrow morning. I blocked the time to spend the morning catching up on e-mail, returning phone calls, and going through the stack of mail accumulating on my desk. Drop by anytime before eleven."

"I'll do that, and thanks. This is important to me."

His heart felt cold and unresponsive. He knew he'd not treated her well, but he couldn't seem to force himself to do the right thing. She'd hurt him, and he wanted retribution. "Sorry, Lord. Change my heart that I might not react in the flesh."

thirteen

Tori headed straight up the stairs to her room and called Jen.

"Hey, girlfriend. What's new?"

"Jake's back and colder than a December frost. I also said good-bye to Spense tonight." Tori fell across her bed, staring at the ceiling.

"Whoa. Never a dull moment, is there? I feel like I need to buckle up and hold on tight every time you call." Jen chuckled. "So, you said good-bye or *good-bye*, good-bye to Spense?"

"Good-bye, good-bye." She liked the confident tone in her voice. This was the right thing for both of them.

"Final, huh? Was he heartbroken? How are you feeling about it? Any regrets?" Jen shot questions at her without taking a breath so Tori could answer.

"It's final, but you know, it felt right. I'm sad, yet peaceful."

"Peaceful's good," Jen assured her. "The question is, does he feel peaceful?"

"More like resigned. He asked me again tonight to marry him, but I discovered through the last couple of weeks that I don't love him in that man-woman way anymore." Tori stretched and yawned.

"I need a scorecard to keep up with you. What about God's will, second chance, and all that?" Poor Jen was behind on her emotional ball bouncing.

"I've really been praying, and now I know Spense isn't who God has for me. If Jake weren't an embezzler, I think he'd be the one, but I'm not marrying a man with that big of a character flaw, nor am I prepared to make wifely visits to a jail cell."

"Did you kiss Spense good-bye?" Jen asked with a romantic edge to her voice.

"Nope, though I think he'd have liked to. But honestly, I'm not even convinced he still loves me. I'm comfortable like an old pair of tennis shoes."

"Shoes, huh? Weird analogy, but I'll play along. Sticking that stinky pair of shoes in the closet, let's focus on Jake. Did you confront him, and what did he say?"

"Not yet. Tomorrow morning I have permission to go to his office. I think I'll get there first thing. Get it over with and come back to my room and pack."

"What will you say?"

"I've no idea, but pray for me."

"So, back to the pair of shoes guy—how are you feeling?"

"In a word—free."

"How so?"

"My pride took a huge hit when Spense walked out on me. As you well know, I was broken and so hurt, but I also worried about what people were thinking and saying. But he came back. Though most people will never know that, I know that. Somehow him coming back vindicates me. Yes, we're still apart, but by my choice, not his. Does any of this make any sense at all?"

"Of course it does."

"And I know the bottom line is that it's all about my pride, and God hates pride. Hopefully someday it will be buried and gone, but until then, I'll still have to deal with the ugly appearances every now and then."

"I disagree. If it were only about pride, you'd not be satisfied with only you knowing it was your choice to end it once and for all. You'd print it in your Christmas newsletter, tell every soul you meet, and maybe even hire a skywriter. I think Spense's return brought you healing that only comes from God, and I think his return grew each of you to be a little more like Jesus. He humbled himself, and you gave him the gift of forgiveness."

"I like your point of view."

"So when will you be back in Tucson?"

"Sunday evening. I spoke to Roni and will be temping at her firm for the rest of the summer."

"How about lunch on Monday? We can meet at HiFalutin. It's in the same parking lot as her firm."

"I'm game. We'll share The General's Favorite Chicken."

"Deal. In the meantime, can I pray for you?"

Her question touched Tori's heart, as Jen's faith often did. "I'd love that."

"Lord, would You be with Tori as she confronts Jake tomorrow? Keep her safe from harm, and protect her. Let her words bring conviction, not condemnation. Prepare Jake's heart. Let him be honest with himself. Break him, and bring him to full repentance and freedom from future stealing. Thanks, Lord, that You use each and every thing for good in our lives as long as we hand them over to You. Do that for Jake. Let tomorrow begin a new chapter in his life. A chapter of living in whole-hearted devotion to You. I lay all this before You in Jesus' name. Amen."

"Amen," Tori echoed, agreeing whole-heartedly with Jen's prayer.

ও

Tori tossed and turned all night. She never fell into a deep sleep. Every time she awoke, all she could think of was Jake and what she would say. Waking nauseous, she wanted to pack, load her little Bug, and hightail it out of there without a word to Jake. Somehow she knew that wasn't the right answer.

Dragging herself from the bed, she showered and got ready. Then she threw open her drapes wide and settled on the loveseat with her Bible on her lap. This year she read five chapters of the New Testament six days a week. That meant she would have read it six times by the end of the year. She hoped the repetition would bury the truths deep in her heart.

At eight o'clock, she stood, inhaled a deep breath, and blew it out slowly. Her hand trembled as she turned the doorknob. Checking her pocket for her room key, she then closed the door behind her. When she got to Jake's outer office, his admin assistant sent her straight back—no questions asked.

She knocked once on the closed wooden door before turning the handle and pushing the gorgeous wood plank open. Jake was seated behind his desk. He glanced up at her. "Come in, Tori."

She did as she was told, shutting the door behind her. She made her way across the plush sage carpet to a pair of wing-backed chairs that faced his desk. Choosing the right one, she settled in, sinking into comfort and style all rolled into one stately brocade upholstered chair.

He watched her but said nothing. Obviously the ball was in her court because he waited quietly for whatever she had to say. He appeared calm, but the pulse in his throbbing jaw belied the image.

Tori cleared her throat and leaned forward.

"I have some concerns."

He nodded. "And they are?"

"You do some things that. . .that don't follow policy." She wiped her sweaty palms on the legs of her capris, glad Jake couldn't see because his desk blocked his view.

"A stickler, are you?" He said it like she was the one in the wrong and not him.

"I believe that rules are in place for a reason, and the number-one reason is that they bring order, which prevents chaos." How did she end up being the one on the defensive, attempting to clarify right and wrong?

"Fair enough. Tell me what your concerns are." He leaned in and gave her his full attention.

"Your weekly reimbursements. The dollar amounts are far more than the receipts. And this week the receipts had to be fraudulent. You weren't even in town!" How she wished she wasn't so emotional during confrontational times. It made her lose credibility.

"Do you think I'm stealing? Is that what you're saying?" His voice was calm, and his eyes squinted some as he watched closely for her response.

"I don't know—are you?" She raised her brows.

"Tori, do you honestly believe I'm a thief?" The way he asked made her feel like she'd made a mistake and he was innocent.

Did she believe him to be a thief? Maybe. Well, if the truth be told, she did. She swallowed hard. How come he was calm and composed and she was terrified and clammy? She stared. What should she say? *Lord, please help me.*

"Well, do you? Is that what this is about? You think I'm requesting reimbursements for a higher amount than I actually spent?"

She nodded. "I went back, and this started four years ago, the same week you hired Allison. You sent Chris to bully her, so she'd turn a blind eye, and she has. Every week—all two hundred plus of them."

His face darkened. "I can't believe this. You think I'm stealing from the resort! I thought you knew me better than that." Disappointment settled over his features.

How dare he be disappointed in her! He was the thief. Shouldn't this be the other way around? Shouldn't she be the disappointed one?

His phone rang. He jerked up the receiver. "Matthews," he yelled into the phone.

Taking a deep breath, he continued in a calmer and quieter tone. "Yes, I did want you to know that I'm having a meeting in my office at three. Can you make it?" He paused. "Great. See you then." He hung up. "Be here at three, Tori." He rose and opened the door, waiting for her to leave. It wasn't a request but an order. *Be here at three.* Well, she would be, but the question was would he? Or would he disappear to save his own skin?

&

As she walked past him, he grabbed her arm and stopped her. "And, Tori, just for the record, you'll be the one apologizing to me."

"I hope so, Jake. I hope so." Her eyes held regret. She grabbed his wrist and loosened his hold on her upper arm.

He closed the door and returned to his desk. "Unbelievable." He shook his head. He'd been right—Tori had figured out the skimming scheme, just not the whole thing. He swiveled his chair around to look out the window.

First Spense and now this. Tori wasn't at all who he thought she was. If she'd ever really loved him, wouldn't she at least give him the benefit of the doubt? He knew he would do that for her. He'd fight to prove her innocent, not fight to hang her from the nearest tree. Jake felt even more betrayed by her than he had before. Choosing Spense over him was painful, but this felt like treason.

He'd say one thing for her. She was sharp. She figured out in three weeks what took Rachel almost four years to see.

⁂

Tori went back to her room and finished packing. She lived and relived her five minutes in Jake's office. Finally, she took a walk and called Jen.

"How did it go? I've been praying all morning."

"You know, I'm out on a walk, and it's finally warming up here. The resort is packed with summer guests. The place is hopping, filled with fun and an air of excitement, and I'm going to miss it all." She ended on a sob.

"Tori, are you okay? Is someone listening to our conversation? You're not really making much sense." She could picture Jen's perplexed expression.

"Sorry. That all just hit me right before you answered. Tomorrow's the day, and I'm not really ready to leave. I'm going to miss the best part of summer, and for what? To go back to the worst part of summer in Tucson and work at my sister's law firm in a job I hate?" Tori settled on a bench. "This is my first day outside without a sweatshirt or coat. The sky is blue." A tear rolled down her cheek. Then another and another.

"I think I get it. All the grief and loss have finally caught up with you. You've been through a lot the last couple of weeks, and to now discover the man you were falling in love with is a criminal. Of course you're upset."

"I don't know, Jen. Jake was adamant that he'd done nothing wrong. He was even angry at my accusations."

"Of course he was. People are angry when they get caught. That's a normal reaction. Think about one of your high schoolers when they get caught cheating. What's the first reaction?"

"You're right. It is anger." Tori used her sleeve to dab her face dry, taking care under her eyes not to smear her makeup. "So back to your original question—it went terrible. He looked so hurt by my accusations that I feel guilty. I mean, I already hurt the guy by letting Spense waltz in and claim me as his own right under Jake's nose. Now this."

"Whoa, whoa, whoa. The guy twisted things, and you're the one who feels bad? Something about this picture isn't right. He's the one who lacks integrity, not you. Don't let him weigh you down with guilt."

"I wish you could have seen his face. I don't know. Nothing makes sense to me. I have no idea who or what to believe." Propping the phone against her shoulder, Tori rubbed her throbbing temples.

"So what now?" Jen asked.

"He asked—" She felt like a liar phrasing it so nicely. "Well, more like ordered me to come to his office at three to find out the truth."

"Don't go." Panic filled those two words.

"I have to." If there was any chance she was wrong, Tori had to know.

"What if it's a trap of some kind?" Tori picked up on Jen's fear—fear she didn't share.

"It's not. It's a meeting of some sort."

"Tori, on *America's Most Wanted*—"

"Jen, you watch way too many crime shows to think rationally. Jake isn't going to murder me and cut me up into tiny pieces and mail you one finger at a time." Those shows were too gruesome for Tori and obviously for Jen, too. They perpetuated fear.

"Please be careful and call me the minute you're through. Promise?"

❧

Jake wondered if Tori would actually show up. By the time she got there, Rachel, Dorie, Chris, and his administrative assistant, Julie had already arrived. Tori entered the office wide-eyed and took the only available seat between him and Julie.

"Thank you all for coming. This will only take a couple of minutes."

Two police officers came through the door without warning. Jake watched Tori closely. Horror filled her eyes.

She whispered in Jake's ear, "I didn't call them."

"I know. I did."

"You're turning yourself in?" Her wide eyes appeared relieved.

"Christopher Corbane, you are under arrest for embezzlement." One officer pulled him to his feet while the other handcuffed him. Then the one that pulled him up read him his Miranda rights.

Tori kept looking from him to Chris and back again.

The arresting officer led Chris from the room. The other lingered until they were out of earshot. He spoke directly to Jake. "I spoke to the district attorney, and the state will most definitely prosecute. Thanks for all your documentation. It should make the allegations stick without a problem."

Jake rose. "I appreciate your cooperation and all those long-distance calls we made back and forth." He shook the cop's hand.

"We'll keep you apprised. From what we can tell, the kid is a recreational drug user, and his salary wasn't as big as his appetite for the next high."

Shaking his head, Jake said, "That's a real shame. I really liked him and didn't have a clue until Rachel brought it to my attention, which was thanks to Tori."

"Pays to keep a close eye on money. It has a way of walking."

"Apparently so," Jake agreed. "We'll rethink our system—that's for sure. We have a payroll clerk, Rachel, an accounts payable clerk, Allison, and an accounts receivable clerk, Dorie. Chris was to supervise the whole accounting operation, which he obviously did very well. If Tori hadn't asked so many questions, Rachel would never have double-checked and warned me."

"That's the problem with having the dishonest guy in charge." The police officer shook his head. "Glad you figured it out and it was a low amount compared to what it could have been. Nice meeting you all. Duty calls." He waved his hat and left the room. Jake turned his eyes on Tori. Her expression held relief and apology.

"I hope to keep this under wraps for several reasons." Jake addressed those remaining at the round table that graced one end of his office. "Chris made a mistake, but I feel his reputation and dignity must be preserved. Let's try not to gossip or slander the man. Yes, people will hear and assume things, but I don't want us to be the ones to carry the tales." He made eye contact with every person at the table. "You are the ones who know what is going on. Also be the ones who keep it quiet. Please." He paused for a moment. "Any questions about Chris or what just happened here today?"

Everyone remained quiet. The proverbial pin dropping was certainly true of this group. "I want to thank each and every one of you for your help in stopping this activity and protecting the resort. And because Chris used his position to scare Allison into cooperating, this will not affect her future with the company. You may return to your work."

Rachel, Dorie, and Julie all rose and left. Tori lingered. She shot him a nervous smile. "You're right. I'm here to eat crow. I was wrong. Can I ask you one thing?"

Jake nodded.

"How did you find out? How did Rachel discover it after this long?"

"Your visit with Allison triggered the whole thing." He glanced at his watch. "I think you caused her to realize the seriousness of the situation, and she didn't want to be party to anything illegal. She called Rachel and tipped her off. Then Rachel did the same thing you apparently did and followed the paper trail. She called me in Arizona and tipped me off. Only she never doubted my innocence." He had to throw that in. "An employee had more trust in me than you did."

She hung her head. "I'm sorry."

"Listen, I have to run. I have a meeting with the board in two minutes."

"Can I buy you dinner? I'd like to finish this conversation, and it's my last night."

He nodded. "Better make it late. I'm not sure how long this meeting will drag out. They won't be happy about this incident and the length of time it went on."

Tori nodded. "How does eight sound?"

"I'll be there. Blue Coyote?"

"See you then." Tori rose, and they walked out together. Dining with her would be the hardest thing he'd do today.

fourteen

"Hey." Jen sounded distracted.

"He didn't do it! Jake wasn't in on the embezzling scheme. I don't know all the details yet, but Chris was arrested this afternoon. That's why Jake wanted me in his office at three."

"Or he turned state's evidence." Jen's explanation threw cold water on Tori's excitement.

"State's evidence?"

"Where one criminal turns on another to save themselves. They make a deal with the district attorney."

"No way. Too many crime shows, Jen, way too many. Anyway, we haven't had a chance to talk yet. He's with the board right now."

"Well, you will know soon enough. Ask him direct questions. Don't let him play you. Dig until you know the whole truth. Honestly, Tori, Chris could be his fall guy."

Tori didn't want to believe anything Jen was saying. "Wait, what happened to his biggest cheerleader? You were the one who couldn't believe Jake could do anything like this. Now there is a chance he didn't. You should be happy for him and me."

Jen sighed. "I'm just saying, the other day on this court show—"

"Enough. You are no longer allowed to watch TV crime or reality shows. Your mind is becoming warped."

Jen giggled. "It's my guilty pleasure. I always secretly wanted to be a lawyer, so I live vicariously."

"Find a new hobby," Tori ordered.

"So now what? Are you still leaving tomorrow?"

"I have to. My sister would kill me if I didn't. As for Jake, we are having dinner tonight. But *since* he's not guilty, that reopens the door to many possibilities, don't you think?"

"If the reason you couldn't be with him has been removed, then yes."

"The reason has been removed." Tori stated it emphatically, but Jen had planted a tiny seed of doubt.

After they hung up, Tori finished her packing and loaded almost everything in her car. She had to make several trips down to the garage. She took extra care getting ready for the evening with Jake. She wanted to look her very best—even wore a dress. Something she rarely did anymore.

At five till eight, she left her room and headed back to the restaurant she'd frequented far too often this past week. It was the only nice dinner spot up here at the top. Driving a half hour to town seemed crazy, so most people ate at the Blue Coyote often.

Jake arrived just as she did, so the host led them to a table for two. Jake pulled out her chair. "I made reservations to avoid a wait."

"I'm glad. When I saw the crowd, I wondered how long it would take to get a table." The host handed her a menu. "Thanks for agreeing to dine with me. I'd understand if you'd rather not." He laid his menu down, and she followed suit.

"If it's any consolation, I am very, very sorry."

"I overreacted out of hurt. I'm sorry, too."

The waiter she'd had twice before greeted them. He gave Tori that knowing look but didn't say anything to give her away. She felt her face grow warm but doubted Jake would notice under the dim lighting.

Jake ordered an appetizer and said they'd decide on dinner in a few minutes. "By the way, the tab is on me."

"But—" She started to protest, but the determined set of his jaw along with the look he sent in her direction quelled any response.

He picked up his menu and studied it for another minute. "Why I look at this thing, I'll never know. I should know it by heart." He laid it back down.

"What's your favorite dish here?" She strove for a normal dinner conversation.

"Depends on my mood. Tonight I'm ordering a steak. I also like the pasta a lot."

"I think I'll try the pasta. I haven't had that one yet." She laid her menu on top of his. Her hand shook slightly. Did Jake notice? His gaze roamed the room, so she didn't think so.

Her heart pounded, and her mouth was dry. She sipped her water. What should she say? Would he understand? Her palms were damp again. She discreetly wiped them on her napkin. He returned his attention to her and smiled. The silence was growing uncomfortable. In his gaze, Tori caught a glimpse of pain. And she was the cause. She hated knowing that.

"Jake, I really am sorry." She looked deep into his eyes, trying to read his thoughts. "And I'm not placing blame, but you are the one who convinced me you were involved."

"Me? How?" He squinted in that endearing way of his when he was examining something closely.

❧

Jake intently studied Tori's face like she was a bug under his microscope and he were a scientist searching for clues. "How did I lead you to believe I was involved in embezzlement when I had no idea it was even going on?"

"By your reaction when I asked about your reimbursements."

"Ah." He remembered the conversation.

The waiter brought their first course, setting it between them. Jake ordered for both of them since she'd already said she planned to try the pasta. When he left, Tori continued, "You were adamant that I pay it and give the check to Chris."

"I'd only learned of it an hour or so earlier in a phone call from Rachel. When Allison called her, she spent the next several days documenting things and putting together a paper trail. Chris had thought of everything. Somehow he even added me to the account at the bank, so all he had to do was scribble 'for deposit only' on the back of each check. Less evidence against him. It was an unused account, which he set up for the purpose of cashing the checks. He kept a couple hundred in there, and no one ever questioned him. He'd deposit the check inside the bank and go through the drive-through and withdraw the very same money on the following day."

He paused to take a bite.

"Why did you nearly bite my head off when I brought it up? That only increased my belief in your guilt."

"I'm sorry. I was afraid for you. I didn't know what Chris might do if you tipped your hand." Clearing his throat, he continued. "As soon as I finished my conversation with Rachel, I called a detective friend of mine who works for the Sandpoint Police Department. He warned me that Chris might get dangerous. Happens more often than not. A criminal is much like a cornered animal—they either fight or flee. Right on the heels of that conversation, you called. All I could think about was how to keep you safe when I was fifteen hundred miles away."

She smiled. "So you figured if you bit my head off that would do the trick?"

He laughed. How he'd missed her sense of humor. "No. I snapped at you out of fear, not thinking how self-incriminating I sounded. Never even dawned on me. Then I willingly accepted your resignation and tried to get you out the door sooner than later for your protection. It wasn't that I didn't want to see you again, I didn't want you in the middle of this."

"Though I still completely betrayed you as my friend, can you see how I ended up there? Your signature was on the weekly PO."

"My very forged signature," he reminded.

"Like I knew that. I even compared it to other things you'd signed. He signs your name better than you do!"

"Yeah, you're right. I checked out some of the documents, and even I would have insisted that was my John Hancock except I knew I'd never signed a purchase order in my life, and Chris knew that. Hindsight and all."

"Leaving the door wide open for him to use that avenue."

"Exactly. And then a week or so later, he really pushed for me to hire Allison over another candidate. I think he saw her as an easy mark. It was obviously a well-thought-out plan. And I have to give you the credit for stopping it. Had you not picked up on the fact that something was going on, this could have gone on forever." He felt disappointed his own staff had missed it.

"You're welcome. It pays to have nosey friends and coworkers. And, Jake, I am so sorry. Heartbroken, really, that I hurt you. That I suspected you. Can you forgive me?"

"Of course." And he did. As they'd talked it through, his anger dissipated. He grabbed a roll and buttered it, finding it hard to keep things so impersonal when all he wanted to do was pull her into his arms and thank God that He kept her safe through all of this. He had done the thanking part over and over, but his empty arms ached to hold her. Except she wasn't his to hold—her heart belonged to another man.

&

He smiled but looked very tired like he had the weight of the world strapped to his back.

The waiter delivered their dinners. Jake prayed and blessed the food. They ate in silence for a few minutes. The whole Spense thing was sitting between them like a giraffe in the room. Now she needed to apologize for that.

"I take it Spense left." Jake sounded so casual.

She nodded, her stomach knotting at the mention of Spense's name. This was her opening since he brought it up. How to begin?

He jumped in before she'd formed an opening sentence. "When's the big day for you two?"

"What big day?" She searched her memory, uncertain of what he was talking about.

"The wedding. Are you going to stick with your original date?"

Dumbfounded, she stared at him. Finally she shook her head. "There is no wedding. Spense and I said our final good-byes last night."

Now he had the dumbfounded expression. "Final good-byes?"

"Final. The end. Done. Over. Through. You thought we got back together?"

"What else could I think? I was there, remember? And I saw you last night, and you guys still looked pretty cozy together."

"Jake, I am so sorry. I don't know what came over me that evening when he showed up in all of his arrogant glory. I couldn't think, couldn't talk. I was so confused. Was he back because that was God's will? I'd prayed for his return for months, and there he stood in the flesh. My brain couldn't wrap around everything, so it shut down.

"I know how that must have looked to you, but it wasn't as it seemed. When we got to my room, I found my backbone and my voice. I informed him we weren't back together. You'd have been proud." She smiled and paused. "I looked for you that night, but you'd already left. I realized how hurt you must have been when I discovered the next morning that you'd left town."

"I should have stayed," he admitted.

Did she have the courage? She forced herself to blurt out the truth. "If it's any consolation, you took my heart with you."

"I did?" He seemed surprised.

"You did."

"So your resigning early had nothing to do with Spense?" Again he studied her intently.

She shook her head. "But it had everything to do with you."

"Me?" He frowned. "Oh. . .because of the money."

She nodded. "Jen convinced me that to stay, I was putting myself in danger as an accomplice. She had me serving jail time and all."

He laughed. "I bet you'd look cute in those orange prison jumpsuits."

"I think not. I'm a summer. Orange isn't my color at all. Makes me look jaundiced."

He again laughed. "I still say you'd be the cutest little prisoner in the place."

Was he flirting? Hope began to seep into her heart. Maybe they weren't as over as she'd assumed.

"Let's recap. You were leaving town because you thought I was a thief. I thought you were leaving town because you were moving forward with Spense. Since I'm not a thief and you're not with Spense, why don't you stay for the rest of the summer as originally planned?"

"I wish I could." With all her heart she wished she could. She filled him in on her upcoming job and her impending death if she failed to show.

"Are you done?" He pointed to her plate.

She nodded. That question came out of nowhere.

"Rick, put this on my tab," he instructed the manager as he walked by. He rose, and she did the same. "Do you have time for a walk?"

"Sure."

They sauntered toward the ski lifts. He seemed to have something on his mind but struggled to say it.

He led her to the seating near the lift. The full moon overhead illuminated the night. They settled on the bench, and he turned to face her. "Tori, I'm sorry I assumed you and Spense were back together. I know I acted like a real jerk several times. Jealousy does that to a guy, not that that's an excuse."

She placed her fingers over his mouth as he'd once done to her. "I forgive you."

He pulled her hand away from his mouth but didn't release it. He smiled at her. "And I forgive you. Stuff this crazy only happens to couples on those corny TV movies."

"Hey, buster, I happen to love those corny movies."

His eyes danced. "So, Miss Wade, you're a romantic at heart?"

Speaking of hearts, hers thudded against her ribs. "I am," she confessed.

"Then let's write a happy ending together."

She nodded. What exactly was he saying?

᠊᠊᠊᠊᠊ ᠊᠊᠊

This wasn't at all how he imagined it would happen. He had no ring to offer, but the timing felt right. He moved closer to her. "Tori, I'm in love with you."

"Still?" He realized she held her breath, waiting.

He didn't make her wait long. "That part of the story never changed. I was hurt and disappointed, but my feelings remained steadfast. I do now and will always love you."

In her eyes he saw his feelings reflected back at him. She laid her hand on his cheek. "I didn't stop loving you either. It broke my heart to think you might be involved in criminal activity, but it didn't change my feelings for you."

He honored his vow not to kiss her passionately again, so he kissed her cheek in several different spots. "Marry me," he whispered near her ear.

She pulled back to look into his face. "Now?"

He laughed. "The sooner the better as far as I'm concerned." Then he grew serious. "I don't have a ring or a plan for the future, but I know it's you I want in that future with me."

"Yes! Yes, yes, yes!" She reined kisses across his face and nose. "I thought I'd lost you to criminal activity." She laughed. "I've never been so happy to be wrong."

"Ditto. I thought I'd lost you to another man and am thrilled to be wrong."

They laughed. What a beautiful sound their blended joy made.

"I love you, Tori."

"And I love you, Jake. When can we seal it with a real kiss?"

"On our wedding night," he promised. "After that, a thousand times a day until forever."

epilogue

May of the following year

Tori followed Roni to the restroom. "Are you okay?"

She heard a sniffle. Then Roni answered, "Yes."

Tori knew Roni was crying, even though the walls of the bathroom stall separated them.

"Don't worry about me. You need to get back to your guests. This is your and Jake's big night before the big day tomorrow." Another sniffle.

Tori ignored her sister's directive. "Roni, what is going on?" She never fell apart, and Tori was more the crier. She hadn't missed the fact that Roni dabbed her eyes all the way through rehearsal and now wept in the bathroom at the rehearsal dinner.

Roni opened the door and slipped out, head hung low. "I'm pregnant. Ashton's only five months old, and I'm pregnant again!"

Tori didn't know what to say. Pulling her sister into an embrace, she hugged her and let her cry.

"Tom's angry. He didn't want one kid this soon, let alone two. And he may not have wanted kids at all." She pulled free, grabbed a paper towel, and dabbed at her smeared makeup.

"Did you guys talk about that before the wedding?"

She shook her head, and regret filled her eyes. "It's been a tough year, Tori. I'm glad you and Jake weren't as stupid as we were and spent a year getting to know each other before you married, not after."

Tori nodded, wishing she'd been wrong about the marriage happening too quickly.

"How well can you know someone in three months?" Roni turned away from the mirror and faced Tori. "Thanks for not saying, 'I told you so.'"

"I didn't want to be right on this one," she assured her sister.

Roni smiled slightly. "Thanks."

"You're going to make it though, aren't you?" Tori was almost afraid to hear the answer.

"Yeah, we'll make it, but it's been hard since day one. We're in counseling at church. Wish I'd listened to you and Mom and Dad. Forever is a long, long time."

A couple of women came through the door and headed for stalls. Roni pulled her makeup bag from her purse and reapplied what she'd cried off. "Mom and Dad don't know yet about this, so keep it on the down low," she whispered.

"Will do." Uncertain if Roni meant the baby or the counseling, she'd just keep both under wraps. Her heart ached for her sister.

Roni smiled at Tori in the mirror. "Go. I didn't mean to burden you with my stuff until at least after the honeymoon."

Tori hugged her sister and then placed her hands on Roni's shoulders. "Tom's a good man. You'll get through this."

"He is." Roni turned toward the mirror and opened her mascara, removing the wand. "We just didn't really know each other very well, and getting to know each other after the fact has added a lot of tension, then throw a baby into the mix and now two. . ."

Tori nodded at her sister's reflection and patted her arm.

"I love you, Roni. Don't forget the power of prayer."

A toilet flushed, and Tori headed for the door. She turned and waved before exiting. Tori plastered a smile on her face, really wishing she could go somewhere and cry for the mess Roni had made of her life.

When she got home that night, she pulled out her journal. So many things to share with the Lord.

Tomorrow's the day. Tomorrow I will walk down the aisle of my church and join my life with Jake's. I love him so, and God, I just have to say thanks. The things that broke my heart last year are cause for celebration this year. Except Roni, of course—she chose a difficult path for herself. But You are a redeemer and can redeem this mess she's in. Do it, Lord, do it—that Your glory may be seen.

Thanks, Lord, that I didn't marry Spense. Jake is so much more than Spense in every way. He's more in love with You, more in love with me, and less impressed with himself. Hindsight is twenty-twenty, and things are sure looking clearer these days. Jake is everything I wished for and so much more. He is tender, giving, and he adores me! I feel loved and don't question or doubt like I did with Spense. What a gift, Lord, what a gift. Thank You!

Will You teach me to be a godly wife? I want to respect him the way a man needs to be respected. I hope to honor him in what I say to him and about him. Make me aware when I'm nagging. I don't want Jake searching for a corner of the roof to find peace. Lord, enable me to be his best friend, advocate, and lover.

Speaking of lover, I'm nervous, Lord. Seems I've waited forever for this and so has Jake. It's exciting, but scary as well. Just be with us, and bless that part of our marriage.

Tomorrow I'll be a bride! Tomorrow I'll be Jake's and he'll be mine. . . .

Tori lay in bed that night thinking about how she'd changed her wedding plans to better suit her and Jake. They were simpler and more traditional, starting with a church wedding. It was sweet to know she'd walk the same aisle she walked as a child when she went forward to share her decision to follow Christ and then to be baptized.

❧

For Jake the day dragged on and on. He felt like the proverbial horse chomping at the bit. He just wanted to get to the church, say I do, and get the honeymoon started. Tori was nervous. He was anxious. He'd waited a long time. A very long time.

Jake glanced at his watch. Tom and Gordy should arrive any minute, and a limo would show up about half an hour after that. They'd head to the church, where he'd finally see his bride! He hadn't seen her since last night. Just thinking about her brought a smile to his face.

Once they arrived at the church, the three of them hung out in the groom's room of the chapel until the wedding coordinator, Amy, instructed them to take their places at the front of the church.

"Do you have the rings?" he asked Tom.

Tom grinned at him. "Yep. They haven't gone anywhere since the last time you asked."

Jake's palms were sweaty. He followed Amy to the front of the chapel and climbed the few steps to the stage. The pastor was already in place. Jake stood on his left and turned to face the audience. Tom took the spot next to Jake and then Gordy.

As soon as they were situated, the music started. Jake's heart rate felt like it doubled. Jen started down the aisle, followed by Roni. Both girls took their places on the opposite side of the pastor. The first chords of "Here Comes the Bride" sounded out. Mrs. Wade stood. The rest of their guests did the same.

And there at the back of the room stood Tori on the arm of her dad. Never had he seen a more beautiful sight. She wore the sweetest smile, and he knew his grin must have shown nearly every tooth in his mouth. Her gaze never left his as she glided down the aisle. They stopped at the bottom of the steps.

"Who gives this woman to this man?"

"Her mother and I do." Mr. Wade spoke loud and clear.

Who gives this woman. He entrusted Jake with one of his most precious possessions in life. Tori's dad carefully lifted her veil and placed a kiss on her cheek. "I love you, pumpkin."

Tears glistened in Tori's eyes. "I love you, too, Daddy." She kissed him back. Then she took a long-stemmed red rose and presented it to her mother, also kissing her cheek. She crossed the aisle and did the same thing with his mother. Then at last she climbed the stairs and came to him.

After passing her bouquet to Roni, she reached out her hands, and Jake clasped them in his own. The pastor said enduring love doesn't just happen—it takes work. That seemed hard to believe at this point. Loving Tori was one of the easiest things he'd ever done. No work or effort required.

Finally, the time came to exchange vows and rings. Then they shared holy communion. They signed their wedding license. At last the words Jake had waited more than a year to hear came. "Jake, you may kiss the bride."

Slowly he moved toward her. Her lips, like ripe cherries,

invited him. When their lips met, it was a symphony of two souls melding together in one beautiful song. He took his time, savoring the sweetness of her lips. When at last they ended the tender moment, the crowd cheered, guys whistled, and Tori's mother blushed.

"And now I present to you"—the pastor smiled at each of them—"Jake and Tori Matthews."

They faced their family and friends. He clasped her hand, and together they descended the stairs and headed down the aisle to the back of the chapel. He led her out into the dark night as the pastor announced the reception over in the Cholla Building. They ducked around a corner.

"Let's try that kissing thing again," he whispered. "I'm not sure we've got it down yet."

Tori giggled and leaned toward him.

After a minute or two, she whispered, "Oh, I think we're doing just fine."

And they were. A perfect peace settled over them. "We kept God first, and His blessings are already abounding."

A Letter To Our Readers

Dear Reader:

In order that we might better contribute to your reading enjoyment, we would appreciate your taking a few minutes to respond to the following questions. We welcome your comments and read each form and letter we receive. When completed, please return to the following:

Fiction Editor
Heartsong Presents
PO Box 719
Uhrichsville, Ohio 44683

1. Did you enjoy reading *Perfect Peace* by Jeri Odell?
   ❑ Very much! I would like to see more books by this author!
   ❑ Moderately. I would have enjoyed it more if

   _____

   _____

   _____

2. Are you a member of **Heartsong Presents**? ❑ Yes ❑ No
   If no, where did you purchase this book? _____

   _____

3. How would you rate, on a scale from 1 (poor) to 5 (superior), the cover design? _____

4. On a scale from 1 (poor) to 10 (superior), please rate the following elements.

   ____ Heroine   ____ Plot
   ____ Hero   ____ Inspirational theme
   ____ Setting   ____ Secondary characters

5. These characters were special because? _____

_____

_____

6. How has this book inspired your life? _____

_____

_____

7. What settings would you like to see covered in future
   Heartsong Presents books? _____

_____

_____

8. What are some inspirational themes you would like to see
   treated in future books? _____

_____

_____

9. Would you be interested in reading other **Heartsong
   Presents** titles? ❑ Yes   ❑ No

10. Please check your age range:
     ❑ Under 18   ❑ 18-24
     ❑ 25-34   ❑ 35-45
     ❑ 46-55   ❑ Over 55

Name _____

Occupation _____

Address _____

City, State, Zip_____

E-mail _____

The Perfect
MATCH

When the local dating service, the Perfect Match, is burned down to the ground, Annie Peterson is determined to find the culprit. But the number of suspects seems daunting. Will Annie find the party responsible before another building is set on fire? Will her son find his perfect match in the process?

Contemporary, paperback, 256 pages, 5.5" x 8.375"

— Hearts♥ng —

Presents

Great Inspirational Romance
at a Great Price!

Heartsong Presents books are inspirational romances in contemporary and historical settings, designed to give you an enjoyable, spirit-lifting reading experience. You can choose wonderfully written titles from some of today's best authors like Wanda E. Brunstetter, Mary Connealy, Susan Page Davis, Cathy Marie Hake, Joyce Livingston, and many others.

When ordering quantities less than six, above titles are $3.99 each.
Not all titles may be available at time of order.